BADMAN SHERIFF

When the citizens of Coopers Creek elect Ned Turner as their sheriff, they are blind to the deadly mistake being made. For Turner is a lawless rogue seeking to exploit the position for his own advantage. It will be left to mild-mannered baker Jack Crawley to set things right. But can he rescue his town from the worst badman sheriff Montana has ever known?

Books by Simon Webb
in the Linford Western Library:

COMANCHE MOON

SIMON WEBB

BADMAN SHERIFF

Complete and Unabridged

LINFORD
Leicester

First published in Great Britain in 2014 by
Robert Hale Limited
London

First Linford Edition
published 2016
by arrangement with
Robert Hale Limited
London

*A catalogue record for this book is available
from the British Library.*

ISBN 978–1–4448–2863–4

Published by
F. A. Thorpe (Publishing)
Anstey, Leicestershire

Set by Words & Graphics Ltd.
Anstey, Leicestershire
Printed and bound in Great Britain by
T. J. International Ltd., Padstow, Cornwall

This book is printed on acid-free paper

1

On a rainy afternoon in the fag end of September, 1859, several men who had not yet imbibed enough intoxicating liquor that day to render them wholly incapable of speech, were sitting in a saloon in Coopers Creek and talking over the forthcoming election for the post of sheriff.

'I tell you now,' said one of the men, 'Ned Turner is a man like us. You see him dealing cards, he is as fond of a drink as the next man and, as we all know, he can surely handle a pistol. Not to mention where that Crawley strikes me as a mean-spirited and narrow minded fellow. I do not recollect when last I saw him with a drink in his hand. Would you want a man like that prowling around, telling folk what to do?'

'I am with you on this, Tom. You

never see Jack Crawley in a saloon. He would rather stay at home reading a book and probably drinking buttermilk. We need a man who knows how many cents go to make a dollar and is well-liked into the bargain. Turner's our man, for a bet. Another thing is where Turner is a good fifteen years younger than Crawley. You want a young man for lively work of this sort.'

A third man, who had not yet taken part in the conversation, lit his pipe and then said slowly, 'Still and all, you need to make sure what you are about. A bad sheriff is the devil for a town. Put your hands on your hearts and tell me that you would trust Turner with your money. Or for the matter of that, with your daughters and wives. Besides which, I mind that there is more to Jack Crawley than first meets the eye. I would not be too ready to dismiss him out of hand.'

There was silence for a space before the first man to have expressed his views spoke again. 'There is somewhat in that. Turner is a sight too ready to play kiss-in-the-ring with another man's woman and I will not deny this. But you can understand a man of that brand. He is one of us. Jack Crawley looks like he has no blood in his veins. I will be voting for Turner.'

'Crawley is a nice enough fellow, I will grant you,' said another man. 'He takes round the plate in church and is always helping folk out and suchlike, but is he the one to stand up to some of the types who are plaguing the town? I do not think so.'

The man with the pipe said the final word before the conversation turned to other matters. 'There is more to being sheriff than just swaggering round with a gun at your hip. There will be book-learning needed for taxes and so on. I doubt that Turner is your man for that.'

Ned Turner and Jack Crawley were the only two men who had voiced any desire to become sheriff of the small town of Coopers Creek in Montana.

The opinion of many in the town was that the life expectancy of the man taking up that tin star would very likely be measured in weeks rather than months. There would be no question of the new sheriff being able to appeal for help to any higher authority; whoever took on the job would be solely responsible for law and order over the whole, entire town and all the diggings surrounding it. It could prove a hard row to hoe and no mistake. Coopers Creek was a rough and ready sort of place and deaths resulting from trifling disputes and drunken quarrels were currently running at the rate of at least one or two a week.

Coopers Creek was one of a dozen or so new towns which had sprung up like mushrooms in the wake of the Montana gold rush. From a huddle of tents and lean-tos, it had grown in a few short years to a sizeable place with everything one could hope to find in a civilized town, such as stores, saloons, livery stables, bakeries, churches and cathouses. All it lacked now was a sheriff; a vigilance committee having heretofore kept order.

While the forthcoming election was being debated in the saloon, Jack Crawley was working in the bakery, which he had started when he arrived in Coopers Creek two years before. Jack Crawley was a taciturn and self-effacing man in early middle age. He was quiet and thoughtful and had never yet been seen wearing a gun; not at all the sort of fellow that most of those in the town could readily imagine keeping order with any great success.

Crawley was kneading dough that wet afternoon on a flour-dusted trestle table, and working at his side was one of his two apprentices: seventeen-year-old Jim Parker. This youth was known to one and all as 'Bony'.

'Well, boss,' said Bony, 'have you really put in your papers for this sheriff business?'

'That I have, son,' said Crawley, continuing to pummel and punch the gooey white mixture of flour and water.

'How do you reckon your chances against Ned Turner?'

'I don't think I have any 'chances' to speak of, I think he will win for certain-sure.'

'Well if you think that,' asked the puzzled boy, 'why are you making a contest of it? What's the point of entering a race that you think you're going to lose?'

Crawley stopped work and eyed his young assistant with disapproval, tinged with amusement. 'What a mercy that the early Christians did not take that line,' he said. 'Our Lord too, for the matter of that. You'd think he would have just said, 'I'm not going to win this contest against the Devil, so I reckon I'd best not try'.'

'Ned Turner ain't no devil!' exclaimed the literal minded Bony Parker.

'Is he not?' replied his employer. 'Well then, I miss my guess.'

While some were getting liquored up

in saloons and others were baking bread, Ned Turner was engaged in the more congenial occupation of seducing another man's wife. To be more precise, he had finished seducing her and was now in the process of getting dressed, ready to run a few card games in the saloon.

'Come back to bed, honey,' said the woman beneath the sheets. 'You know Donald won't be back until tomorrow.'

'That's nothing to the purpose,' said Turner. 'I have to show my face around town tonight, not to mention letting a few of them suckers win at my table.'

'You are going soft in the head. Why you going to let folk win?'

Ned Turner looked serious for a moment. 'Because with that election coming up, I want people to feel better disposed towards me than they are liable to if I have took all their money from them at cards the night before they are due to vote.'

The woman in the bed laughed, a deep, rich, throaty chuckle. 'You think that playing fair for a few nights is going to make everybody forget how you rooked them in the past?'

'Folk have short memories. A lot of those boys spend their whole lives getting cheated, one way or another. They ofttimes forget who cheated them or when it happened. Your husband is a fine example of the breed.'

'Nobody ever cheats Donald at cards, nor at business neither if it comes to it,' she began and then giggled. 'Oh, I see what you mean. I suppose that you could say he has been cheated this very day.'

'All I purpose is to let a few men have good wins at the table this night, which will have the effect of blotting out the recollection of all those other nights when they have left without a cent. I know men, trust me. They will remember the winning and forget all the losing in the past.'

Donald Sefton's wife sat up in the bed, pulling the sheets around her modestly. 'You don't really think folk round here will vote you in to be sheriff, do you?'

'I am convinced of it. Would you want that Bible-reading milksop of a baker to run the town? People might not altogether trust me, but they know that I am a man who can handle things. They will vote me in.'

'You won't be able to run card games in the saloon if you get to be sheriff. It will not be what people want. Anyway, why do we suddenly need a sheriff? The vigilance committee has managed all right 'til now.'

'Card games!' exclaimed Turner contemptuously. 'There are bigger fish to fry in these parts than card games. I just about make enough out of cards to keep me in liquor and cigars. I will not get rich in that way.'

He buttoned up his shirt and buckled on his gunbelt. 'As to why we need a sheriff, the town has just got too big for a vigilance committee to handle; a handful of vigilantes will no longer answer. Besides which, there will be permits to issue, licences to collect payment for, a whole heap of things. It will be a full-time job.'

'And you're the man for the job, I suppose?' said the girl mockingly.

'You got that right!' said Turner. He leaned over, kissed the girl hard on the lips and left.

* * *

The election was due to be held on the first day of October, which was a Saturday. Being a suspicious bunch, nobody in the town quite took to the idea of a secret ballot and so the election was to be decided by a public show of hands. There being no suitably large public building for the purpose, it was agreed to stage the voting in the larger of Coopers Creek's two saloons. The candidates were to make speeches to the assembled crowd, following which the vote would be taken. The general feeling, both in the town itself and out at the diggings, was that Ned

Turner was a shoo-in for the job.

The night before the election was marred by the very sort of incident that went to show the need for a sheriff. Two men, who were, by-the-by, tolerably close friends when sober, had fallen out over a woman. Nothing else would do but that they must fight to the death over the lady's affections. The chosen weapons for this affair of honour were Bowie knives.

The duel took place back of the saloon, just after dark, with the scene lit only by flickering pine torches. Now, the state those two men were in from drink, it is something of a wonder that they could stand upright, never mind fight. Howsoever, they managed to cut each other to pieces. The supposed winner stood triumphantly over the body of his vanquished adversary, roaring his success. Then he too collapsed in a heap from blood loss, and not fifteen minutes later he expired. Folk said that this was the first such fight that they had seen for a good long spell that resulted in the death of both combatants.

By the time that Ned Turner stood up to deliver his speech on the Saturday night most of those in the saloon had had a few drinks and were becoming boisterous. Turner didn't mince his words.

'You all know me. I am a man who has his faults, which I freely confess. I like a drink and am not against kissing a pretty girl from time to time.'

Somebody called out from the audience, 'You only kiss 'em, Turner?'

'Well, that's how a gentleman generally begins, at any rate,' said Turner, which brought a roar of laughter. 'But I want to be serious for a moment. Only last night we saw two men die needlessly, just a few yards from this very bar-room. I tell you now, it makes me sick at heart to hear of such goings-on.

'I promise you all that if I become sheriff, I will straighten things out in this here town and that the streets will be safe for women and children. I like the inside of a saloon better than the outside myself, but there is a sight too much drunkenness and fighting going on lately.

'Also, I shall deputize others and we shall end the attacks on the stages carrying the gold from this area. Vote for me and you boys will see some changes round here, that I promise you.'

There was cheering and stamping of feet at the end of Ned Turner's speech and he bowed to the audience. Men said to each other that you knew where you were with a man like Turner. He didn't put on airs and graces and he was just like them at heart.

Jack Crawley stood up and the hubbub subsided. Crawley was a slight figure of a man, his skin pale from working indoors all day at the bakery. He looked slow, serious and old.

'I am not a one for fancy speeches. Before you vote, you need to think over one or two things. Have any of you thought about the money to be made out of being sheriff of this town? About how much will be charged for permits to build or various taxes? How all this money will be tallied up and used correctly?

'Whoever you give this job to had better be good with bookkeeping as well as able to shoot straight. Not a one of you has ever heard of me cheating anybody or trying to put something over another man. You need to think well on all this.

'If you give me the job, I can tell you that I will do it to the best of my ability, on behalf of all of you. You had best choose a man you know to be honest and not just one who can shoot fast and straight. That's all.'

There were a few half-hearted claps after Jack Crawley sat down, but it was plain that those in the saloon were not overmuch interested in hearing about bookkeeping. They wanted a tough fellow who would lick the rowdier elements into order. Ned Turner was elected by a very sizable majority. Crawley shook his opponent's hand after the count, looking at him queerly in a way that Turner did not rightly care for. Almost, he thought later, as though Jack Crawley, that whey-faced little baker, could see into his heart and knew what he was about. Turner was all joviality to his defeated rival.

'Will you stay and have a drink with me, Jack? Just to show there are no hard feelings?'

'Thank you, no. I do not touch ardent spirits.' He carried on looking searchingly at Ned Turner's face, at which that man became a little tetchy.

'What is it? Do I have a smudge or something on my nose?' he asked a touch irritably.

'No,' said Crawley, 'It is nothing of the kind.'

'Well, what then? Why are you staring at me like that?'

'I hope,' said Jack Crawley slowly and with obvious sincerity, 'I hope that I am wrong about you.' Then he turned away and walked out of the saloon, a thoughtful and troubled look upon his face.

'Snot-nosed bastard,' muttered Ned Turner. 'I can't stand a sore loser.' He soon put the strange little baker out of his head entirely and gave himself up to celebrating his victory with an extended drinking session, which did not end until three the next morning.

Jack Crawley walked home with a heavy heart. As soon as he entered the house, his wife began to condole with him, under the mistaken apprehension that he was disappointed at not being appointed sheriff. He laughed when she hinted at such a thing.

'You think I *wanted* to give up that bakery and let those two muddle-headed apprentices of mine run the place into the ground? Not a bit of it. I stood only because I could see the town running headlong into foolishness. Ned Turner, indeed! I never heard the like.'

'Are you sure that he is as bad as you represent him to be?' asked Josie, his wife. 'Is it not possible that you are doing him an injustice?'

'What can I tell you? He is a drunkard, an adulterer, a liar and a cheat. Is this the character we would hope for in the man who is to be responsible for the law here?'

'Perhaps it will work out all right,' said his wife, trying to soothe things over. 'Sometimes, men grow into responsibilities of this sort and give up their old ways. Perhaps this will be the case with Ned Turner.'

'I hope so, but I doubt it. There is something more to the case, that I cannot quite put my finger on yet. God forbid that I should judge any man harshly, but I fear that there is more wrong about that man than even I suspect.'

* * *

Despite the heavy drinking of the night before, Ned Turner was up and about bright and early the next morning, preparing for what he conceived to be his new duties. The former vigilance committee was now calling itself the 'citizens' committee' and was hoping to transform itself into something like a town council. Turner had it in mind to corrupt the key men in the new council and bring them under his influence, so that rather than he being their employee, he would instead have the whip hand over them. But first, he had business out at some of the older diggings, a spot near the river which had been pretty much worked out.

A tumbledown collection of wooden shacks was strung out along the base of the river cliff. It had become a kind of shanty-town, full of squatters and drifters. Turner approached on horse-back at a cautious walk. As he was almost within hailing distance of the huts a man emerged without warning from the trees and bushes to his right. He was cradling a shotgun in his arms and when he saw Turner he raised it to his shoulder, as though preparing to fire. Spotting the star pinned to Turner's shirt, he said, 'Well, well, looky here! So now we have a sheriff in these parts. That is just fine.'

There was a pause of a second or two, before the man's face split into a huge grin and he lowered the gun, saying, 'Ned, you old cow's son. Sure is good to see you. So you did it? You really did it? Lord God, this must be the first town I ever heard tell of which voted in a road agent as its sheriff.'

Turner scowled. 'Hush your mouth, you damned fool. Where are the others?'

'Scattered round. You want to speak to everybody?'

'I surely do, Ike my boy. The good times are coming for us. I wanted you boys to be the first to hear the news. Between me and my associates, as you might call them, we are going to squeeze that little town dry.'

2

On the afternoon of Wednesday, 5 October, large bills appeared in various prominent places around Coopers Creek, affixed to walls in the saloon, general store and livery stable, as well as pasted up on the outside of a number of buildings. Neatly hand printed, by the wife of a man who owed Ned Turner a favour, they read:

Take Notice!!!
Fighting, Riotous behaviour, Discharging Firearms & Public Drunkenness Are Now Forbidden in the Town of Coopers Creek Offenders are liable to be imprisoned for twenty-four hours and face Unlimited Fines

Signed N. Turner
(Sheriff of Coopers Creek)

The general view of those reading these notices was that this all seemed very feeble and unlikely to inhibit to any serious degree the rowdiness and high spirits which were disrupting the peaceful life of the town. The vigilance committee had administered some severe beatings, cropped one thief's ears and hanged two men in the last year. Notwithstanding these measures, there was more violence than ever in Coopers Creek. Some opined that Ned Turner must be a deal softer than had previously been supposed. Twenty-four hours' imprisonment indeed!

At dusk one miner decided, on the urging of his friends and after a few hours in the Tanglefoot saloon, to put the matter to the test. This man, Tom Barker by name, left the saloon and stood in the middle of the street. He then proceeded to pull out his pistol and fire it firstly into the air and then at the sign hanging above the livery stable. He had fired off four shots, when Ned Turner arrived on the scene. Now you could say many harsh things about Turner and he was indubitably, as Jack Crawley had observed to his wife a few days earlier, a cheat, liar, drunkard and adulterer. One thing you could not accuse him of, though, was a lack of courage.

The newly appointed sheriff nodded affably to Barker and walked up to him slowly. 'Did you not read my notice, concerning the discharging of fire-arms?' he asked mildly. And then, before the drink-befuddled fellow had been able to frame a coherent reply, Ned Turner pulled out his own gun and slammed it into the side of Barker's head. This mighty blow from a two-pound chunk of steel did not achieve the desired effect and so Turner struck him again a couple of times, whereupon Tom Barker dropped like a pole-axed ox.

There were murmurs from some of Barker's friends, who had followed him from the saloon to watch the fun. The new sheriff turned to face them, his gun still in his hand.

'Anybody wanting a similar sort of treatment?' he enquired in a friendly tone of voice, as though offering them a glass of whiskey. He found no takers and so holstered his pistol and then bent down to the unconscious man lying at his feet. He took a hold of Barker's belt with one hand and his collar with the other, then heaved him up like a sack of potatoes and slung him over his shoulder. Then he set off towards the blacksmith's place.

Back of the forge there was a stout wooden shed with a sturdy door. It was only ten feet by six and had no windows, just a ventilation grille up at the top by the roof. Ned Turner had got the citizens' committee to rent this small structure from the blacksmith. That morning, before putting up the posters, he had furnished it with a chamberpot.

When he reached the shed Turner dumped Tom Barker unceremoniously on the ground and went through his pockets. Like quite a few of the prospectors thereabouts, Barker carried with him the gold that he had panned in a leather pouch. The sheriff weighed the little bag in his hand and calculated that it contained perhaps a quarter of a pound of gold. He also found a little over twenty dollars in cash money in the man's pockets and confiscated that as well. Then he unbuckled Barker's gunbelt and heaved the still senseless man into the shed, locking the door after him.

Until a proper sheriff's office could be built Turner was just working out of the room he rented. After locking up Barker he went back there and made a few calculations. Then he headed off to the home of the former head of the vigilance committee, who was now the nominal leader of the new town council and perhaps soon-to-be first mayor of the town. This worthy greeted Ned cautiously, wondering what was to do.

'Well, Jim,' said Turner in a sad and

sober voice, 'I'm afraid I have to tally up the reckoning this day of all that you owe me. I'm sorry to have to do it, but I have my tail in a crack now, having taken on this job. I cannot run any more games, and so I am calling on all those who owe me money to make their settlement. I have your notes of hand here over the last nine months and it all adds up to nigh on a thousand dollars. Nine hundred and eighty-eight, to be exact.'

Jim Kincaid was appalled. He had been playing at Ned's faro table pretty regularly and had been given credit on various occasions, signing chits which Ned Turner handed to him when he was pretty well liquored up. Kincaid operated his little store on a damned fine profit margin and there was not the slightest chance of his being able to raise $1000 to pay these debts at a moment's notice in this way.

Ned Turner knew perfectly well that Kincaid was stumped. He had been preparing for this moment for months and now the time had come to reel in the fish.

'I surely do not like to come down hard upon you, Jim,' said Turner. 'Still and all, I am out of pocket here to a considerable extent. I do not know what to suggest. Unless . . . No, I don't think a man like you would go for such a scheme.'

A flicker of hope flared in Kincaid's heart. A minute earlier he had been facing the prospect of ruin; maybe of having to sell his store in order to settle up with Turner. Not only could he forget about becoming the first mayor of Coopers Creek, he might have to leave town altogether. Nobody likes a man who welshes on gambling debts. He seized eagerly upon the hint that there might be a way out of this embarrassment.

'Tell me what's in your mind, Ned. If you can see a way out of this, I will never let it be forgot.'

The time had come. If he had miscalculated the weakness of the man standing before him, then Ned Turner would himself have lost everything and probably have had to start from scratch in another town. He pulled out the leather pouch containing the four ounces of gold which he had taken from the drunk whom he had just recently locked up for the night.

'This here is around four ounces of gold, the market price of which is currently twenty-one dollars an ounce. This is the amount we are fining the fellow who I arrested earlier for firing his pistol off in public. I will deliver all such fines to you and you will reckon them up. I suppose you plan to use such money for the good of the town, in a civic way?'

Jim Kincaid and the other members of the former vigilance committee had not really thought this far ahead, but now that Ned put it so, it all sounded very right and proper.

'What I would suggest to you, Jim,' said Turner, 'Is that you skim twenty-five per cent off the top of these fines, for your own use. Then you can repay me when you have got straight yourself. Of course, if the idea does not suit, then we can just settle up now . . .'

The moment when an essentially honest but weak and fearful man is corrupted and changed into a thief often passes unremarked, either by the man himself or those around him. So it was with Jim Kincaid. He knew that what Ned was proposing was crooked but, after the awful prospect of losing his livelihood and home, taking a portion of the fines exacted in the town seemed to be the lesser of two evils.

'Only you and me would know of this; right, Ned?'

'Of course. Why would I say a word to anybody?'

'And you would hold back on those IOUs?'

'Hell, Jim,' said Turner in a sincere voice, 'I don't want to make things hard on you. You're one of my best friends.'

Manoeuvring the head of the town council into being indebted to him and also getting him into a position where Turner could at any time expose him as a thief, was the first stage in neutering those who were supposedly his employers. After leaving Kincaid Ned Turner went to see another member of the council. He told this man that one of the girls in the cathouse whom he had been screwing around with had become pregnant and that he, Turner, had arranged the abortion. He just wanted the fellow to know about it so that he knew there was nothing to worry about.

The story about the abortion was a complete pack of lies. Turner had heard from one of the girls that this man had been sneaking in to the cathouse and the idea of the pregnancy came to him as an inspiration. As he left the grateful man, Turner winked and said, 'Don't worry, I won't say a word of this to your wife.' Then he was gone.

Until Ned Turner had said this, it had not occurred to the fellow for a moment that Turner *would* say anything to his wife. Now he started thinking and came to the conclusion that it would be a mighty fine idea to stay on the right side of Ned Turner in every way that he could.

Before he went back on duty that evening, Turner had one final call to pay. This was to another member of the citizens' committee and this time there was no need for any chasing round the woodpile; he just told the man straight, without mincing his words. Turner had discovered that this man had committed an unnatural act with another man. He put the case in this way:

'You are one filthy devil, you know that? What would folk think if they was to hear about this? One place I knew, out in California, they tarred and feathered a fellow for that and then ran him out of town. Another place, they beat the men concerned so badly that one of them died.'

'Ned, you got to believe me, it was just the once. I ain't never done anything of the kind before or since.'

'I don't give a shit about that. Listen

now and I will tell you how the matter stands. As long as I am the sheriff of Coopers Creek, why, you have nothing to worry about. But I will tell you this. If, for any reason at all, that council of which you are a member ever decides to dispense with my services, then it is all up with you. I will tell everybody in the town what you were up to. You believe me?'

'Yes, yes I believe you. And thank you.'

'Don't thank me. I got your pecker in my pocket, as you might say. You tell me every damned thing that those men on the council get up to, what they say, what they do, who they're screwing: the whole works. That clear? And you better argue hard against anybody who feels like they don't want me to be sheriff any more.'

Having ensured that three of the town council were either indebted to or scared of him, Ned Turner returned to his patrol. That first night he caught two men fighting and one making water in the middle of the street. He relieved all three of all their money and locked them up in the shed at the back of the blacksmith's place. Altogether that night, he had acquired eleven ounces of gold and eighty-six dollars in cash. He kept two ounces of gold for himself and fifty dollars in bills and coins. The rest he intended to pass on to Jim Kincaid the next morning. In effect, he had made himself ninety-two dollars for three hours work. It was a good beginning.

A week later some of the town's menfolk were shooting the breeze in the saloon.

'Well, I reckon that Ned Turner has done what he promised. The streets are a sight quieter than they have been for a year or more.'

'I could not argue with you there. Nobody wants to spend twenty-four hours locked up in that dark shed with an overflowing chamber pot and perhaps a man being sick everywhere. It surely acts as a deterrent.'

An older man said slowly, 'What, though, of those men who claim that Turner robbed them of considerable sums?'

'Like the signs said: 'unlimited fines'. And Ned Turner is not sticking to that money himself. He is passing it on to Jim Kincaid and it will be used for the benefit of the town. When all's said and done, if you behave decently and don't make trouble in the streets, you are not likely to lose any money. Those who fight and so on are purely asking for trouble and if the sheriff obliges them, well that is their affair.'

At about the time that this conversation was taking place in the saloon, Jack Crawley was sitting down at table with his wife and twelve-year-old son. Crawley said to his son, 'Would you like to say grace, Albert?'

The boy bent his head, closed his eyes and said solemnly, 'For what we are about to receive, may the Lord make us truly grateful. Amen.'

Jack Crawley and Josie echoed the

'Amen' and the family began to eat. After a space, Albert said to his father,

'Pa, is it true that the new sheriff is keeping the town safe and stopping bad men from hurting us?'

'Who told you so, son?' asked Crawley. It was a peculiarity of Jack Crawley's that he treated his son pretty much as he would have done an adult person; listening carefully to what the boy said and answering all his questions as well as he was able, and freely admitting it when he did not have enough information on the case to express an opinion.

'The boys at school say that since we have a sheriff, there is less fighting and drunkenness. They say that we have law and order now.'

'What do you think, Albert?'

'What I cannot make out is, when Mr Turner says that some person is drunk or fighting, who is to say that he is right? Seems to me that he is acting as policeman and judge both.'

Jack Crawley smiled at his son. 'You

have touched the matter with a needle, son. It is Ned Turner's rightful duty to catch those suspected of breaking the law, but deciding upon their guilt and perhaps punishing them is the job of a court.'

Josie broke in at this point. 'You cannot deny, though, that the town is quieter and more respectable since we had a sheriff. You know it to be true, Jack.'

Jack Crawley looked fondly at his wife. 'It is well and good now perhaps, although I guess that there is some thievery taking place already. What about when Turner sets his attention to people like us?'

'But Pa, you are not going to be getting drunk or fighting. Why should the sheriff trouble you?'

'I will tell you this, Albert, and you too, Josie. Within a fortnight Ned Turner will be trying to get money out of other people in the town apart from lawbreakers. I have seen this before and I know how it goes.'

Josie and Albert stared in bewilderment at Jack Crawley, unable to imagine how any sheriff could possibly be aiming to target such an obviously upright, God-fearing and law-abiding man as he.

Ned Turner had moved into a suite of rooms above the Tanglefoot saloon. He could afford to: after only a week his new job was raking him in over $500 a week on top of his salary. It was there that he was entertaining Ike Holbeech, who was still living out at the abandoned diggings and had come to town to urge Turner to make it possible for the men at the diggings to move into town.

'What you need to understand,' explained Turner patiently, 'is that robbing a whole, entire town in this way takes considerably more preparation than knocking over a bank or holding up a stage. I have spent nine months readying the ground and do not wish to screw it all up now by moving too fast. Have you forgotten how haste spoiled our chances in California?'

'Yeah,' said Holbeech, a mite too truculently for Ned Turner's taste, 'That is all well and good, but while you are riding high on the hog here in town, the rest of us are living in wickiups and mud huts like a bunch of damned beggars. The boys are getting restless.'

'Are you saying that you could run this business better than me?' asked Turner bluntly. 'Do you say you want to take over the enterprise?'

'No, I am not saying that. But still and all . . . '

'Must I needs remind you and those others that until you picked up with me, you were all scraping a living hand-to-mouth by robbing lone travellers of their watches and wallets? You were starving when I first picked up with you, Ike; don't you attempt to deny it now.'

'There is somewhat in that. We just want to know when we can come into town and join in the fun, as you might say. Don't take on so, nobody is challenging you.'

'That is as well,' said Turner. 'You at least can move here in the next few days and the others may follow at intervals. Everything is now in place. You will be my first official deputy.'

Ike Holbeech's face lit up. 'You mean that I shall be a proper lawman again? It will be like Redemption all over again.'

'I hope not,' said Turner. 'Do I need to remind you how fast we had to leave there when things went wrong? I hope that we manage it better this time. Come on, I want to introduce you to a couple of members of the citizens' committee or 'town council' as they are wanting to be known now.'

Abe Calthorpe was the undertaker in Coopers Creek and also belonged to the citizens' committee. Although married, he had a liking for muscular young men and it was this that had given Ned Turner his hold over the man. Calthorpe had been varnishing a coffin in his workshop when Turner walked in with another man whom Calthorpe could not recollect ever having seen before. Turner did not feel the need to disguise his true character when talking to Calthorpe, and so he just said at once what he expected from him, without beating around the bush.

'See this man?' asked Turner. 'I want you to vouch for him to the other members of your council and say that you know him to be an upright, honest and reliable sort of person. His name is Ike Holbeech and I propose to make him my deputy.'

Holbeech was a short, flabby, overweight man approaching middle age. His face was not unintelligent, but there was a mean look about him which made Abe Calthorpe feel distinctly uneasy.

'I'm not sure about this, Ned — ' began Calthorpe, whereupon Turner cut in with the utmost ferocity:

'You damned sodomite, don't you go

telling me that you ain't sure about something. I am telling you now that you will vouch for Ike here and say that you knew him years ago. You will further tell your friends on the council that he is honest and trustworthy.'

'Well, I guess — ' said Calthorpe.

'You'll do more than guess, you son of a bitch. You had better make a strong case as well to your friends, because I tell you now that if they do not agree to this man being my deputy, then I will see that you ride out of town on a rail. Is that clear?'

Turner and Holbeech left without waiting for a reply.

* * *

In the last week Ned Turner had arrested twenty-nine people for various offences against public order. All had spent twenty-four hours in the increasingly filthy conditions of the old blacksmith's shed. In addition to this, every one of them had been relieved of all the cash and gold that he had been carrying. Turner had taken a flat rate of twenty dollars for himself from every one of the men, giving him $580 over the course of the week. The remaining $1,700, mainly in gold, he had handed over to Jim Kincaid. Assuming that Kincaid was skimming a quarter of that, the town was left with an income of $1,200 that week, about which none of the town council could complain.

There were signs that some of the miners and prospectors were aware of how they were being skinned and that some at least were not prepared to put up with this barefaced robbery for very much longer. This was why Ned Turner felt that it was time to bring some of his old gang into town to support him when things turned rough.

The folk in the town itself were happy enough with the way that Coopers Creek was being managed by their new sheriff. It was nothing to them if a few drunken and troublesome types were being locked up in squalid conditions, and even less if they were being forced to pay out around $80 a head in gold for the privilege of spending the night crammed three or four at a time into that filthy hole. Nobody could deny that things were getting quieter in Coopers Creek: that, after all, was why they had hired themselves a sheriff in the first place.

3

Twelve days after Jack Crawley had predicted that Turner would soon be setting his attentions to the more respectable citizens of the town there were two visitors to the bakery. Ned Turner and Ike Holbeech came in, as friendly and amiable as you like, just to pass the time of day; or so it seemed at first.

'Jack, I thought I would just introduce you to my deputy. Ike, this here is Mr Jack Crawley, who provides the town with its bread. A most valuable service.'

Crawley nodded to Turner and Holbeech. He did not smile at them or invite them to sit down. Turner had something more to say.

'You probably heard how we are now straightening up this town and making it a fit place for families to live in. You are a family man yourself, Jack, I am sure you have noticed how there are fewer drunks and no fights at all lately?'

Jack Crawley still said nothing, just eyeing the other men calmly, waiting to see what would come next.

'Now the thing is,' said Turner, 'we are needing to raise money for various improvements that our new town council has in mind. I don't rightly know all that they purpose, but it seems fair that we all contribute in our various ways. As sheriff, I have the responsibility for collecting the taxes and suchlike, which is not going to make me popular.' He laughed. 'Still, this is not business. What it amounts to is this. I am drawing up a schedule of what the stores, saloons, livery stable and other places like that should be paying towards the upkeep of the streets, civic amenities and so on. Now I have assessed your share as sixty dollars a week. Ike here will collect it every week from now on.'

Jack Crawley watched Turner and

Holbeech with no expression at all upon his placid and good natured face. At length he said, in an even and unemotional voice, 'Are you putting the bite on me?'

Ned Turner looked horrified. 'Jack, Jack, I don't know what I can say! I am only following my instructions from the council. They want to set up such things as a fire service. This will cost money, but you can see the sense in it. Why, just look at this place. You have that oven burning away in a wooden building here. It would only need a spark to set the whole place alight. Not only would you lose your business, but other buildings might catch afire too.'

There was an uncomfortable pause, during which Crawley stared apprais-ingly at the others.

He said softly, 'I will think on this and let you know later what I have decided.'

After the sheriff and his deputy had left Jack Crawley took off his apron and left his apprentices in charge of the place for the morning. He strolled down the street to the undertaker's shop. Although he was not a particular friend of Abe Calthorpe the two of them had always got on well enough together and, since Abe was a member of the town council, Crawley thought it worth while to get his fix on this matter of taxes. After greeting the other man and passing a few general remarks about business and the weather, he went straight to the point.

'What is all this about taxes, Abe? I had Turner and his new deputy in my place just now, telling me that they wanted sixty dollars a week from me. You're on the council; what is all this about?'

'Why are you coming to me about it? I know nothing of it.'

'Where does that deputy come from? I heard where you gave him a character and that this was one of the reasons that he was engaged. Where did you come to know a man of that brand?'

'Jack, don't go making waves, you

hear me now? Just pay up the money like the rest of us are going to do.'

'The rest? You mean it's true and that all the businesses round here are being hit in the same way? What are you paying?'

Calthorpe was sweating, his face drawn and white. 'What does it matter to you what I am paying? Nobody will thank you for rocking the boat. Now if you don't mind, I have work to be doing.'

'What are you scared of, Abe? Has Turner or that man of his been threatening you?'

'Nobody's been threatening me,' snapped Calthorpe. 'You're just making a damned nuisance of yourself, Jack Crawley, and creating problems where there weren't none before.'

Calthorpe made a great show of getting on with his work and ignoring the presence of Crawley, who stood there watching him thoughtfully for a spell. Then he turned and left the shop. It was plain as a pikestaff to him that there was some mischief afoot and that, just as he had suspected all along, Turner was using the post of sheriff not for the benefit of the town generally, but rather to line his own pockets.

Opinions in the Tanglefoot saloon were still in Ned Turner's favour. It was undeniably true that the streets were more peaceful since his appointment, and the word was that money was now flowing into the town's coffers; money which would be used for the improvement of Coopers Creek.

'I mind that those prospectors are getting a little tetchy about the level of the fines that they have been paying lately,' said one fellow, a day or two after Turner had demanded sixty dollars a week from Jack Crawley. 'Still, they have a remedy in their own hands. If they don't cut up rough at night and disturb the peace, why then, they will not be arrested and fined.'

'That is true,' said another man. 'I do not have patience for those who complain about such things. If folk don't fight and create trouble, why, they will not have to spend the night in the lock-up or lose their money.'

Some of the prospectors were indeed becoming 'a little tetchy' about the fines that were being exacted from them. There was good reason for this. Although there were still a few rowdy types whom Ned Turner was legitimately locking up for the night, there were others whom he was taking into custody for quite another reason.

* * *

Since it would not have looked quite right to have the sheriff running the faro table in the saloon of an evening, Turner had invited one of his cronies into town to operate the games on his behalf. This person was as skilful as Ned Turner himself in rigging the dealing box so that the banker had a greater edge than would otherwise be the case. Despite this, some of the gamblers still managed to win tidy sums at the table. The chips were valued at either ten or twenty dollars and so it was not uncommon for a man to walk away with a couple of hundred dollars profit. When anybody had an especially good win of this sort another of Turner's friends, who hung around the table just for this very purpose, went off to alert the sheriff.

What brought matters to a head was the events that had taken place the previous night: the night before Turner and Holbeech had called on Jack Crawley at his bakery. One of the miners had started with a relatively modest stake of two ten dollar chips, which he purchased with an ounce of gold dust. He then proceeded to win the astonishing sum of $580, all starting from those two chips. This proceeding almost broke the bank and the man running the table was sick at heart to see so much of his money leaving the table.

Rather than play on until he had lost the lot, this fellow cashed in his chips and left the saloon with almost $600 in cash.

Amazing to relate, the man who had won all that money was not a drinking man and so, when he encountered Ned Turner and Ike Holbeech on a dark stretch of the road, he was as sober as the proverbial judge. Having already been tipped off by the man who hung round the faro table, the sheriff and his deputy were waiting for the lucky winner.

'Hold up,' said Turner, as the fellow approached, 'Don't you know that public drunkenness is no longer tolerated in this here town?'

'Drunkenness? What in hell are you talking about? I have not touched a drop of liquor in almost three years. Now move aside.'

While Turner and the miner were talking in this wise, Ike Holbeech had moved round behind the man. He plucked the pistol from the man's holster and then gave him a mighty push, which sent him staggering in his effort to remain upright. He turned angrily to see who had assaulted him, only to hear Ned Turner say, 'You ain't touched a drop of liquor? Just look at you, you can hardly remain on your feet. Staggering round all over the shop. You'd best come along quietly with me now if you know what is good for you.'

As the sheriff finished speaking, Holbeech brought his pistol down hard on the back of the man's head, sending him sprawling in the dirt. Turner then followed up with a couple of well-aimed kicks. Between them, they bundled the dazed erstwhile winner along to the blacksmith's. There, they rifled his pockets and took every cent they could find, before locking him in the stinking shed for the night.

When the miner was released, an hour or so after Jack Crawley had been pressed for money, the man went straight back to the diggings and told his story to a few friends. Since he was known as a sober and hard working man, the idea that he had been arrested and fined $600 for drunkenness did not go down over well with his friends. It was decided that a deputation would visit Coopers Creek that very night to make their dissatisfaction known in the strongest way.

* * *

At dinner that evening Jack Crawley was thoughtful and subdued. His wife asked him outright what was the matter.

'What ails you, Jack? Do not say 'nothing', because that would not be a truthful rendering of the situation. I know something is amiss.'

Young Albert chipped in. 'Tell us what's what, Pa. I am old enough to help you with it, whatever it is.'

Crawley looked fondly at his wife and son. 'I cannot deceive the either of you for a moment, it seems. Very well, I shall speak plainly, but on one condition. That is that neither of you breathes a word of what I say outside this house. Is that agreed?'

Josie and Albert agreed and so Jack told them of what had happened when Ned Turner and his deputy came to see him that afternoon.

When he had done so, his wife said, 'But perhaps there is something in this, I mean about a fire service and all. Perhaps the town council will really be using money to improve the town.'

Crawley laughed shortly. 'It has improved pretty well over the last couple of years without anybody skinning me for sixty dollars a week. This is a racket. They talk of new services for our town, but what they have in mind is taking the money for their own advantage.'

Albert looked shocked. 'You don't mean that Mr Kincaid from church is a thief? He is the leader of this council, isn't he?'

Crawley spoke slowly. 'I do not say any man is a thief, which is a terrible accusation to lay against anybody. I say that thievery is afoot and that at least some in the town council are involved. I do not know which of them yet.'

Josie caught that little word 'yet', and asked fearfully, 'Jack, tell me that you are not about to do anything that might put in hazard your business or our home. It is not to be thought of. Can you afford to pay sixty dollars a week?'

'I can afford to pay that sum, yes. It will not stop there, though. It will be sixty dollars this week and then seventy the next. It will not end until whoever is at the back of the thing has taken all our money from us. I told you, it is a racket; a trick to rob us under a threat.'

Josie and Albert looked worried, hoping that whatever was happening would not involve Jack Crawley to any large extent. There was silence for a few seconds after he had spoken, a silence which was broken by the sound of gunfire from the centre of town.

As soon as darkness had descended upon Coopers Creek a party of seven men had ridden into town, their intention being to recover the money which Ned Turner had been taking in 'fines'. Apart from the man who had lost $600 the night before, all the others had been taken for between $75 and $250. The seven of them were armed to the teeth and ready to raise Cain if it meant retrieving the money that they believed had been stolen from them.

Relations between the miners and prospectors and the townsfolk were a little prickly. Although it could not be doubted that the gold being dug up was bringing prosperity to Coopers Creek, it was also bringing drunkenness and disorder. Those in the town were thankful for the trade, but not desirous of the rough ways of those who seemed to have plenty of wealth to dispose of.

That being so, it was unlikely that anybody in town would take the part of those miners in any dispute with the sheriff. So far, Ned Turner's depredations had been more or less limited to robbing men from out of the town and because he had kept his promise and made the place quieter, most folk in Coopers Creek were feeling pretty well disposed towards him.

The seven men tethered their horses outside the saloon and went off in search of the sheriff. Turner was in his rooms above the bar-room. He knew that some species of trouble was bound to result from his actions the night before. This had been the first outright theft that he and Ike had undertaken and he knew at the time that it was liable to provoke a crisis.

Ned Turner would sooner have the crisis come at a time of his own choosing and so he had made his preparations for the little drama which was now unfolding outside his window in the street below. He had had fifteen minutes' warning of what was about to happen, when one of his men still living out by the old diggings rode in and told him and Ike what was afoot.

As a consequence of this forewarning, Ike and another of Turner's gang were both positioned on rooftops overlooking the main street. A lot would depend upon their shooting skills, but Turner had had too many proofs of that in the past to feel uneasy on the subject. He needed to focus fully upon the sawn-off twelve-gauge and made his way downstairs.

In the bar he caught the eye of the man running the faro game, who nodded and then covered the table to cries of protest and dismay from the players. Four on seven was good enough odds, especially when the four were Turner and three of his gang. Unless he missed his guess, all that those miners would have was bluster and brag. It was to be doubted that any of them were halfway near as proficient with firearms as Turner and his boys.

Now the fact of it was, there were quite a number of people in the town watching the confrontation as it developed. This meant that the sheriff could not simply follow his natural inclinations and shoot the bastards down from cover, without giving them any sort of chance. His position was not yet secure enough for that. He would have at least to give the appearance of fair play.

As has before been remarked, Ned Turner did not want for courage. He walked out of the saloon and took his stand in the middle of the road, some twenty yards or so from the group of angry men.

'Well, boys,' called Turner to the men. 'What will you have?'

Now it was a new moon and the area outside the saloon was pretty much in darkness, there being nothing in the way of street lighting. One or two buildings had oil lamps hanging in front of them, but it was hard to see who was who or what they were doing. All that those hardy citizens who were peering into the street saw was their sheriff fronting a group of armed men on horseback.

In short, Ned Turner looked to be doing just precisely what the town paid him to do; which is to say standing up to troublemakers and those who would breach the peace.

When they caught a sight of him standing there, there were shouts of recognition and the group began to move towards him. At this point, Turner shouted in a right loud voice, 'Hey put down that weapon! There is no need for violence.'

Right on cue, Ike fired at the saloon, shattering a window and sending the sightseers clustered there fleeing for their lives. At that first shot, all those townsfolk watching the drama ducked or threw themselves to the ground. It was at this point that Ike and the other man on the roof opened up with their rifles.

The second after the first shot had been fired Turner and the faro dealer dived for cover and began firing into the confused mass of men. The miners began firing back and a regular gun battle ensued.

Those inside could not know of the two men with rifles who were picking off the miners from a high vantage point. As far as they knew, it was just the sheriff and the fellow who ran the games in the saloon, taking on Lord knows how many desperate gunmen who seemed to be intent on shooting up their town.

When the firing ceased five men lay dead. The remaining two men had fled and Ned Turner emerged as a hero, having taken on a bunch of wild men who started shooting first. Memory is a strange and unreliable thing and all those who witnessed the events of that evening would have taken oath and sworn in a court of law that Turner just stood out in the open and was fired upon first.

There were some who had been watching him and the card-player and they could swear that neither made a move until the bullets started flying. Those five men who died had brought their deaths upon themselves and no blame could be attached to the sheriff.

At 3.30 a.m. in the morning after the gunfight, a strange sight would have been seen by anybody who was up and about in the vicinity of the saloon. Not that anybody was around at that ungodly hour, so nobody spotted the town's baker climbing through the broken window at the front of the saloon. He carried a candle and once inside the dark and deserted bar-room, spent ten minutes methodically searching the room. He examined the grimy walls and then began to sweep the sawdust aside, looking closely at the wooden floor.

In the end, Crawley found what he was looking for; a ragged hole gouged in one of the planks. He had brought a pocket knife with him and he used this to dig around the hole that he had found. It took a while, but he eventually managed to extract a shapeless and squashed chunk of metal from the wood. He gazed at it for a few seconds, before climbing back out of the broken window and going home.

Once he was back at his house Jack Crawley lit a lamp and studied the misshapen lump of lead, which was about the size of a pea, in close detail. He fetched a watchmaker's glass from a cabinet and stared at the thing with satisfaction, mixed with a terrible foreboding.

4

The day after the shoot-out both Ned Turner and Jack Crawley were feeling pretty satisfied with themselves, although in very different ways. Turner was exulting in the fact that he was riding higher than ever in the estimation of the town's citizens. He was now able to represent himself as the man who stood alone against the forces of violence and disorder; as the saviour of Coopers Creek. It would be a rash man who would challenge his authority now, at least for the time being.

Over at the bakery, Crawley was feeling that grim satisfaction that one feels when worst suspicions are confirmed and you realize that things are every bit as bad as you feared them to be. Jack Crawley was not exulting in this though: quite the opposite. He had listened to the accounts of the previous day's affair and knew without the shadow of a doubt that nobody knew what had really happened. Nobody that is, except he himself.

The lump of lead that he had dug out of the saloon floor was a minie ball, which could only have come from a rifle. The fact that it was embedded in the floor of the saloon and not the wall, meant that it had been fired downwards at a sharp angle; most likely from a rooftop. Since everybody agreed that the shattering of the saloon window was the first shot in the gunfight and, it was popularly supposed, had been caused by one of the miners firing a pistol at the sheriff, Jack Crawley was now certain-sure that the accounts of what had occurred were mistaken. Somebody had triggered the shooting by firing a rifle downwards into the saloon window. The fight had not been started by the miners. Ned Turner had been out in the street and claimed that the miners had started shooting at him first, which made it clear that he was lying. The only question was: what to do next?

* * *

Bony Parker was in a chatty and conversational mood.

'Did you hear about that shooting last night, boss? They say that five of those villains were killed.'

'Why do you call them villains?' asked Crawley.

''Cos the sheriff was just standing there with that fellow who runs the faro table. Just the two of them, facing a dozen gunmen. Then they opened fire. I heard where somebody got cut by flying glass when the window in the Tanglefoot got shot out. They say Ned Turner never batted an eyelash. Just started shooting back until the bad men ran for it.'

'You don't want to believe all you hear, Bony,' said Crawley. It was instructive listening to Bony Parker's version of events, which was probably the one now circulating generally throughout the entire town. Gallant Sheriff Turner takes on the bad men single-handedly. New sheriff routs band of gunmen trying to kill him for no reason at all.

It was the stuff of legends and would serve only to enhance Turner's standing in Coopers Creek. It was time to look a little deeper into this business, decided Crawley.

'Bony, you think that you can run this place this morning and get everything into the oven on time?' asked Jack Crawley.

'Sure boss. What's happening?'

'Nothing's happening. I have to pay a few calls is all. Try not to burn down my bakery or anything while I am gone.'

* * *

Jim Kincaid was busy with paperwork when Crawley arrived and did not seem disposed to chat.

'Jack, I am right snowed under with work this day. Can it wait until tomorrow?'

'It cannot.'

Kincaid sighed. 'Very well, what's on your mind?'

Crawley took the minie ball from his pocket and handed it to Kincaid. 'What do you make of this?'

'It's a bullet, I guess. What's your point?'

'It's a rifle bullet, a minie ball.'

Jim Kincaid looked more closely at the little lump of lead.

'Happen you're right. So? Listen, Jack, I am in an awful rush today, so could you get to the point?'

'I found this embedded in the floor of the saloon, nigh to that window that was broke during the shooting last night. Nobody said anything about anybody using rifles during the ruckus, and even if one had been fired in the street, the bullet would have gone through the window and struck a wall. That first shot, the one that smashed the window and triggered all the firing, came from up high, most likely on a roof. It was fired from a rifle. That gun battle was a put-up job and Ned Turner is lying about the whole affair.'

There was dead silence after he finished speaking and it struck Jack Crawley that Kincaid did not seem to be in such a mad hurry any more to get on with his work. It also struck him forcefully that Kincaid did not seem to be overmuch surprised at what he had said. At length, the other man said:

'That is the hell of an accusation you are making. Some might think that it is because you are still sore at Ned Turner being made sheriff instead of you.'

At this, Crawley laughed outright. 'That what you think, Jim? You known me long enough, you really think that I am a man of that stamp?'

'No, I don't say so myself, but there are those who would.'

Crawley observed Jim Kincaid narrowly for a second or two and then said, 'I went to see Abe Calthorpe just the other day. He was scared out of his wits and gave me the bum's rush. You had the same air about you when I came here. Are you scared of something as well, Jim?'

'Can't you just get on with baking bread? Are you trying to get some exemption from the new business tax? I will speak to Ned Turner and we will reduce your assessment to some trifling amount such as one dollar or something. Will that get you to back off?'

Jack Crawley stood up and shook his head slowly. There was sadness in his voice when he said, 'Jim, you have been got at. I do not know the details or what Turner has on you. Something in the gambling line, I shouldn't be surprised to learn. But the truth is, you are not the honest man you once were and I am sorry for it.'

* * *

There were eight men in Ned Turner's suite of rooms above the Tanglefoot.

Apart from Ned himself, there was Ike Holbeech, the man now running the faro table and six others. They were tough, capable-looking men; the sort of fellows that you felt it would not be healthy to get crosswise to.

This then was Turner's gang. These were the men who had been preying on the stages carrying the gold from Montana down to Salt Lake City; just as a few years earlier they had, under Ned Turner's leadership, been robbing stagecoaches in California during the gold rush there.

One thing that nobody in Coopers Creek, excepting these men alone, knew, was that this was not the first time that Turner had been appointed sheriff of a gold-rush town. Back in 1856, when he had been just twenty-three years of age, Ned Turner had managed to get himself made sheriff of the small town of Redemption, in California. Just as in Coopers Creek, there was not what you might call a great rush of people wanting that job.

Turner had noticed that during a gold rush some men get wealthy and others become poor. You might think that it was the men who found gold who became rich and those working at humdrum jobs in town who stayed poor, but this was not at all the case. Those who found the gold were often fiddle-footed young men who would throw away their newfound wealth at a game of cards or by buying drinks for everybody in a crowded saloon.

The real beneficiaries of the gold rush were often enough those in town who ran the saloon or provided other services for the prospectors. This was why, although they had robbed a few stages, Turner felt that fleecing a town of its profits might be a better bet.

It took Ned Turner and his friends a little over six months to get a tight grip on Redemption and begin to bleed it dry. As well as being sheriff, which meant that he and his gang were able to extort taxes and levy high fines, Turner and his men had been mixed up in various other rackets. Unfortunately, they had become too greedy and the town rebelled against them. Ned Turner and his gang barely escaped with their lives on that occasion, leaving the area only a step or two ahead of a lynch mob.

After Redemption, there had been a leaner time, when the gang had even split up for a while, but now that Ned Turner was securely ensconced as sheriff again in a boom town, it looked like the good times were back again. This time, Turner was determined that they would not rush things and that skinning Coopers Creek was a long-term enterprise which he and his boys could undertake at their leisure, once they had their feet well and truly under the table, as one might say.

Now that he was sheriff, what Turner needed was men who would assist him in his plans; men who knew what he was about and were not likely to be troubled to any great extent by their consciences. Which accounted for the gathering in his suite over the saloon.

Ned Turner held up a Bible and said, 'I am swearing you five men in as peace officers. Repeat the oath after me.'

The man running the faro table could not with propriety also be a deputy and so it was agreed that he would just keep on at that activity, sharing the proceeds of the table with the others.

* * *

Jack Crawley wandered round the town, visiting the barber's shop, livery stable and even the saloon. Everywhere he went, he heard the same story. Ned Turner was the best thing that had happened to the town in ages. He was young, smart and knew how to handle a pistol. There was no telling what would have been the consequence if he and his friend had not been there to stand up to that gang of ruffians who fetched up outside the saloon the night before. It was plain that nobody would be wanting to hear anything said against their sheriff.

It was not until later that day, after Crawley had returned to his bakery, that the first murmurs of discontent were being voiced about Ned Turner's actions. Two things occurred that day to cause the first misgivings in the minds of some of the citizens of Coopers Creek.

At about four in the afternoon, a new set of bills were posted up around the town by some rough looking types wearing deputies' stars. These posters read as follows;

Take Notice!!!

The carrying of firearms of any description in public is forbidden throughout the whole town of Coopers Creek from October 26th. Those violating this law are liable to be imprisoned for twenty four hours and also face unlimited fines. This is an emergency measure, taken in response to the recent disturbances and will be rescinded as soon as possible.

Signed Ned Turner
(Sheriff of Coopers Creek)

Many men at that time only felt fully dressed when they had a gun at their hip. Although most respectable citizens seldom fired the things, they were a sign that those carrying them were free and independent men, able to hold their own against all comers. The notion that men might now be forbidden under penalty of law from wearing pistols was a novel and displeasing one.

In the saloon there were now two topics of conversation, neither of them favouring Ned Turner. One was the new ordinance banning weapons from being worn in public and the other the appearance of half a dozen rascally-looking types who had seemingly been appointed as deputies.

'There is something strange about this business,' said one man, as he sipped his drink. 'Why has Turner not made deputies of some men in the town? Who are those vagrant-looking characters who are now marching around with stars on their shirts?'

'I am minded to go over and ask Jim Kincaid what the score is,' said another man. 'He is supposed to be in charge of this citizens' committee or town council or whatever the hell it is called. He is over and above Ned Turner and should be able to countermand any orders that Turner is now making. Meaning, that is to say, those touching upon the carrying of firearms in town.'

'I never heard anything of the sort, before.' said the first man. 'I can see the sense in banning some of those prospectors and suchlike from toting iron in town, but not those of us who live here. I vote we stroll over to Kincaid's place and ask him what the Sam Hill he is about.'

It was agreed by the four men sitting round the table that they would, after the next drink, go and see Jim Kincaid.

* * *

Jack Crawley was back working in his bakery, having finished his perambulations around the town that morning. He had sent Bony Parker and the other boy off for the day and so was alone when Turner walked in, accompanied by two men who looked like they would be well suited to appearing on some Wanted bill relating to extorting money with menaces or robbery with violence.

Crawley stopped work and faced the three men. Ned Turner did not dress up his intentions beneath soft words on this ocassion, feeling as he did more sure of the strength of his position.

'I hear where you have been bothering Jim Kincaid. That will not answer. Kincaid and me are of one mind when it comes to what is to be done in this town. Do not attempt to sow division between us, it will not work.'

'What do you want, Turner?' said Crawley. 'I am a busy man. Busy, that is, in the sense of providing a service for others, over and beyond beating folk up and robbing them. If you take my meaning, that is.'

'Yeah,' said Turner, 'I take your meaning well enough. Now you listen to me, Crawley. I have my eye on you. So do my deputies. If I catch you trying to cause trouble again . . . Well, I had better not catch you a-doing of it, because I am apt to get vexed if I hear or see anything of the kind again. Do we understand each other?'

'I think you and me understand each other just fine,' said Crawley. 'I understand that you are a thief and a liar and you for your part understand that I am an honest man who will not put up long with such goings on. Is it this that you meant when you asked if I understood you?'

'Just keep out of my business, Crawley. That's all. I will not ask you again so pleasantly.'

* * *

While Ned Turner and his boys were putting the frighteners on Jack Crawley, four men were sitting in Jim Kincaid's front parlour, unable to figure the play. The four of them had all known Kincaid for years and knew him to be a regular, decent sort of fellow. He was a churchgoer, but not a prig like Jack Crawley, who would not gamble or drink. All those present had seen Jim in the saloon, supping whiskey and playing faro. None of them could figure out what he was about now.

'The thing is, boys,' Kincaid said, 'We need to stop all this shooting and violence from running out of control. That is why Ned Turner says, and I agree with him, that just for a week or two it would be good if the only guns floating round the streets were those in the hands of peace officers.' He spread his hands in an open and honest way, like a man who had nothing to hide. 'I don't like the idea any more than you do. Hell, I usually carry a piece myself when I'm out and about, but there it is.'

'Who are these new deputies?' asked somebody. 'Why could Turner not have deputized men from the town, men we know and trust?'

'Oh, that!' said Jim Kincaid, easily. 'There is no mystery there. That Ike Holbeech is well known to some members of the town council and these are people that he and Turner vouch for. They are a lively set of fellows, if a little rough around the edges. It is a hazardous job, taking on some of those roughnecks from the diggings, and I don't think many people would want to do the job and run those risks for what we are paying. You should be grateful to those men.'

Although there was nothing that anybody could rightly put their finger on, something about Kincaid's spiel rang false in the ears of all four of the men who had gone to see him. They left his house not a whit more satisfied and reassured than when they went in.

When Jack Crawley had finished up for the day at the bakery he went home, observing with displeasure the bills announcing that in a few days time nobody would be allowed to carry weapons in public. It was one of those things that sounded right sensible and designed to protect ordinary citizens, but meant in reality that only those of an evil disposition would be armed and that they would be able to enforce their own authority upon the town by force of arms.

* * *

When he got home Crawley took a short ladder from the shed by the side of the house and used it to gain access to the loft. His wife and son were not at home, which suited him well just at that moment. He pulled the ladder up after him so that he was not likely to be disturbed by anybody and had complete privacy. Having hauled up the ladder he also replaced the trapdoor, so that nobody would know he was up there.

The loft was illuminated by a small round porthole window at the front of the house. The place was full of the usual sort of junk that people store in such places: broken furniture, old crockery, and various boxes and trunks. Jack Crawley pulled out one long trunk and dragged it to the window so that he could examine it at leisure. The lid was not fastened and so he lifted it up to reveal clothes and faded newspapers.

He smiled as he read the front page of the paper on top of the pile. It was dated 5 March 1847 and featured an account of the battle of Buena Vista, which had been a pivotal event in the Mexican War.

Beneath the old newspaper was a commemorative print: a steel engraving showing a scene from the battle. At the lower corners were two miniature portraits. One was General Taylor, who went on to become President of the USA. The other was of a young captain of the artillery. Under this picture were the words: *Captain Jack Crawley — the*

Hero of Buena Vista.

Crawley laughed. 'Hero of Buena Vista' indeed! He had never heard such nonsense. He recalled as though it were yesterday the grim struggle against Santa Ana's army. Crawley had been in command of a battery of field guns which held the key to the whole campaign. If he and his men could prevent the reinforcements from reaching the main battlefield, then the Americans would be the victors. Otherwise, it would be all up with them and the whole war might be won or lost on the strength of that one battle.

Twelve years later, and he could still remember every detail of that day. Major-General Zachary Taylor riding up to him, a lowly young captain, and telling him that he had to hold the position on the heights at all costs and halt those reinforcements in their tracks. He had told the general that his fire did not seem to be slowing down the advance of the Mexicans, whereupon Taylor had given the command that became famous across the whole nation when he stood for president the following year.

'Double-shot your guns and give them hell, Crawley!' the general had ordered and this was just exactly what Captain Crawley had done. From that time onwards, the general was known to one and all as 'Give 'em hell Taylor'. Those were the days!

Mind, it had not been all glory and medals and it was the suffering and pain that he witnessed during Buena Vista that decided him to quit his career in the army and train for a quieter and less bloodthirsty trade: that of baker.

Crawley lifted out the rest of the contents of the trunk. There was his old uniform, including his sword and, right at the bottom of the trunk, his pistol, one of the first Colt Walkers. He took it out and hefted it in his hand.

The pistol was just as heavy and satisfying as Crawley recalled. It weighed over four and a half pounds and took a heavier charge than any other handgun of the time. It was said, although he had never seen this tested in real life, that the killing range of the Colt Walker was in excess of a hundred yards. This was a special model and engraved on the smooth cylinder were the words, *February 23rd 1847 Captain Jack Crawley — the Hero of Buena Vista*. His men had presented it to him when he left the army.

There was a holster too; not some fancy gun-slinger's rig, but a standard army holster such as any artilleryman might wear. There were also moulds for bullets and a few other bits and pieces. Crawley opened the trapdoor and lowered the ladder, taking the pistol and other accessories with him.

* * *

Over at the Tanglefoot Ned Turner was running into trouble, not from the townsfolk but from his own men. He tried once again to explain the situation.

'You all know why we had to dig up and light out of Redemption so fast. It was pure greed that did it. We killed the golden goose. Had we been patient and just set quiet a little while longer, why we could still have been there until this very day.'

Ike spoke for the others. 'Yes, that's all well and good, begging your pardon, Ned, but we have been setting out in that shanty town, while you have been living it up here in town.'

There were murmurs of agreement from the other five men. It was a good thing that Turner was paying top rates to rent those rooms at the Tanglefoot, because the state that his men were reducing the furniture and fittings to was a pure disgrace. Upholstery was being torn by their spurs, there had been spitting of tobacco juice on the carpet and even wiping of noses on the drapes at the window.

'Listen,' said Turner again, beginning to lose patience. 'We are now all comfortably established here. I do not want to move out in a hurry, not with winter setting in and all. I hope that we shall still be living in nice warm lodgings when next spring comes round. This will not be the case if we let things get out of hand.

'After we've enforced this ordinance about the bearing of arms we must back right off and not put any more pressure on the town for a space. I do not know how long; maybe a month or so.'

'What we going to do for money until then?' asked one of his new deputies.

'We have the money coming in from fines and so on. Then there is the profits from the faro table. I shall make sure that this is all shared out fair. There is a lot of money to be made here, but we must take it slow.'

'Yes,' said another of the men, 'You may well say this, situated as you are in this luxury. My room at the boarding house is not like this place and I have so far received only forty dollars. I reckon we need some more cash money now.

To hell with waiting a month.'

'Truth is,' said Ike Holbeech to Turner, 'we are all pretty much of the same mind. We think that we should hit the stage the day after tomorrow.'

Ned Turner choked in amazement. 'Why, you jackasses, it is not to be thought of. You must all have taken leave of your senses. I told the people when I was voted in that I would put a stop to raids on the stagecoaches. What do you think it will look like if one is knocked over just after I have acquired six deputies? They will say that I am not doing the job for which they elected me. No, it is out of the question.'

Even as he said this, Ned Turner knew that it was hopeless. He had spent nine months establishing himself here and now it was all going to be blown away because his men were greedy for whiskey and girls. He was consumed by helpless anger. If he did not manage to bring them round to his own way of thinking, then it would be like Redemption all over again.

5

It was the morning of 25 October, the day before the prohibition on the carrying of firearms was due to come into force in Coopers Creek. Neither Ned Turner nor those in the town who were angry and discontented about the business knew what was going to happen on Wednesday 26 October. If everybody just flat disobeyed him, then Turner would be finished in the town. He and his little crew could not fight against the whole town. If he got his way though, it would mean that he and his men could spend a leisurely winter plundering Coopers Creek more or less to their hearts' content.

It was a big 'if' though, and as if that were not enough, Ike Holbeech and the others had made it plain to Turner that they were going to hit the stage whether or not he was with them. He could not fight against them; they were, after all, the prop and stay of his strength here.

While the sheriff was wrassling with his own dilemmas Jack Crawley and his family were sitting down to breakfast. It was one of those gloriously bright but chilly days one gets up in Montana at that time of year. The sun was shining like it was high summer and the trees had not yet shed the last of their leaves. Crawley was in a jovial mood, very different from the way that he had been in general since the election for the sheriff. After Albert had gone to school, Josie turned to her husband.

'You had best be straight with me, Jack. What is afoot?'

Crawley began to say something cheery and reassuring, but she silenced him with a gesture.

'Do not tell me that nothing is going on. I am your wife. Tell me what is in your mind.'

Her husband sat there with his coffee

cup in his hand, not speaking for fully a minute. Then he said, 'Ned Turner is a damned villain and I have it in mind to put a stop to his games.'

'You? What is it to you? You are not a member of the citizens' committee. To put the case plainly, you are the town baker. What is it to you that you need to sort this affair out?'

'I was not always a baker, Josie. I was not a baker when I met and married you.'

'No,' she said passionately. 'You were a man of blood. Fighting and killing the Lord knows how many men. You do not need to remind me of that. I had hoped that times had changed since those days.'

Crawley spoke slowly, trying to set his words in line with the thoughts that he had lately been having.

''All that is necessary for evil to triumph is for good men to do nothing'. If we do nothing now, then Ned Turner and his hired guns will take over this town and loot it. Why do you suppose that they do not want ordinary citizens to bear arms?'

'I do not know that it would be a bad thing if people stopped bearing arms. You have yourself told me of the needless loss of life when two drunken men settle their disputes with guns rather than fists.'

'It depends if everybody is without guns. If only bad men have them, then I do not see that as an improvement on the present arrangement.'

Josie looked at her husband, fear and exasperation showing in her face. 'What then are you hoping to do? Tell me straight.'

'The first thing I shall be doing is buying some black powder for that pistol of mine.'

The woman looked at Crawley in horror. 'Tell me, Jack, that you are joking about this? You cannot really mean to arm yourself at a time such as this.'

He stood up, walked over to his wife and put his arms around her. 'Josie, I am a peaceful man who wants nothing more than to bake bread for the rest of his days. You know this to be the truth. Howsoever, I cannot sit back and watch this set of rascals skin the town in which I live.

'I do not need to remind you that five men were only recently slain here and I have good reason to believe that it was an ambush laid by that man as calls himself the sheriff.

'It would not sit easy with my conscience to see more such actions being taken, with me just minding my own business and baking loaves of bread as usual.'

Seeing that there was nothing more that she could say to dissuade her husband from the course upon which he was set, Josie said, 'Well then just take care that you do not get your own self shot. You are no longer a young man and it must be over ten years since you handled a gun.'

Crawley smiled. 'That is why I want the powder. I shall ride out into the hills and see if my old skill has not completely deserted me.'

* * *

At about the same time that Jack Crawley left his house to buy black powder for his old pistol, the sheriff had come to a decision in his mind. If the stage was to be robbed, and it was clear to him that, either with or without his aid, that was to happen, then it would be best if he supervised the operation and minimized the harm that this rash action might otherwise cause to his own plans.

There was no assay office in the Montana gold-fields at that time, the nearest being 500 miles away in Salt Lake City. It was to that place that large amounts of gold were dispatched by stage once a week. For their day-to-day needs many of the miners and prospectors used gold as it came. In the saloon, for instance, a pinch of gold dust between thumb and forefinger would buy a shot of whiskey and an ounce would buy two ten-dollar chips at the faro table. Larger nuggets though, were sent to Salt Lake City to be assayed and sold. This was a tricky and uncertain undertaking, due to the fact that there was no sort of insurance operating around that part of the country for journeys of that kind.

Gold was packaged up and addressed to the assay office, where some of the men had accounts to which the proceeds of the sale would be credited. If however the stuff were to be stolen en route, then they stood to lose everything. True, the stagecoach companies took every precaution, with men riding shotgun and even engaging outriders and flankers to escort the coaches at times, but there was still regular loss from the attacks by road agents, more commonly known as highwaymen.

When once he had eaten his breakfast in the saloon, Turner went in search of Ike Holbeech. When he had tracked him down he suggested that they take a turn together, walking beyond the town and out of the reach of any listening ears.

'Is it then the case, Ike,' asked Turner, 'that you and the boys are determined at all costs to pursue this foolish track? By which I mean robbing the stage as it travels near here?'

'Ned, if we just make this one raid, then I promise you that after that we will do as you say and set quietly for a space,' said Ike. 'You must admit, you are doing better than the rest of us, as regards lodging and money to spend.'

'I thought you at least had more brains than this, Ike, I did truly. Still and all, if you are resolved upon this course of action, then at least let me set the thing up.'

Ike knew when to give way graciously and said at once, 'Ned, you are the leader and always have been. You may plan the affair as seems best to you.'

'You never were a squeamish sort of fellow, Ike. I take it that you have not acquired any scruples lately? You have not got religion or aught of the sort?'

'It is not likely,' said Ike. 'But no, I have not taken to visiting the church nor am I worried about who gets injured in the course of a robbery. Why?'

Turner had stopped and was gazing back at the town thoughtfully. 'I will tell you. Even if we have bandannas round our faces and hats pulled low and suchlike, there is still the chance that somebody might recognize one of us. You or me being the most likely. For that reason, I propose that we do not leave anybody alive. We shoot every living soul in and about that stage. This includes passengers. As you know, it is not uncommon to find women and children travelling so. If we rob that stage tomorrow morning, we must make sure that there remains alive no witness.'

Ike Holbeech was a violent and unimaginative man, but even so he was appalled by this scheme.

'Everybody, Ned? You mean even if there might, as it were, be some little girl in the coach, we will kill her as well?'

'Yes,' said Turner. 'That is exactly what I mean. No witnesses. We will all of us hang if this miscarries, as well you know. It is madness to operate like this near a town where we are known, but if you and the boys will have it so, then we take no chances. We kill every living soul.'

'So be it,' said Holbeech, but not without some misgivings in his heart.

* * *

There was a little glass display case of guns in the general store. In addition to the usual things such as lamp oil, spades, bolts of cloth, seed and so on, the store also sold powder and shot for such as required it. When the baker came in that morning the storekeeper greeted him amiably as befitted a quiet, sober and industrious man who dealt there pretty regularly for his day to day needs.

'It surely is a fine day, Mr Crawley. What can I be getting you today?'

'Do you have any fine-grained black powder?'

'We do. Is it for a pistol?'

'Yes it is.'

The storekeeper looked at the baker curiously. 'I did not have you pegged for a shooting man. I don't recall that I have ever seen you with a gun of any description.'

Crawley smiled. 'I have it in mind to take up a new hobby. I thought that target-shooting might be just the thing.'

'Tell me, do you have a pistol, or . . . ' the man indicated the glass case.

'No, I thank you. I have a weapon of my own. All I really need is a flask of powder and some caps. You stock caps too, I suppose?'

'We surely do. Do you have your pistol with you? I ask, because some caps fit looser than others. It's good to try them out first.'

Reluctantly, Jack Crawley withdrew

the heavy pistol from where he had tucked it in the top of his pants, under his coat. The storekeeper's eyes widened in surprise.

'You don't want to be starting out with a pistol like that. That's a Colt Walker, it weighs a ton. Mind if I have a look at it?'

The man reached across the counter and took the pistol. Then he noticed the engraving on the cylinder and squinted at it.

'You were at Buena Vista, Mr Crawley? I don't recollect hearing that you were in the army.'

'It is not a thing to be particularly proud of, killing other men for a profession. I try not to think about it.'

'I reckon then that you might know more about guns than I do. I am sorry if I sounded a fool earlier. No offence meant, I'm sure.'

'None taken. Now about that powder?'

* * *

In Ned Turner's quarters he and his six deputies were talking over the finer details of the projected raid on the stage.

'We will need a good reason why all seven of us go riding out of town tomorrow morning and then return after the stage has been robbed,' said Turner. 'The people in this town might be a little simple, but they are not completely mad. They will form a connection between the two events and if that happens it will without a doubt be just like Redemption all over again. With the possible difference that this time we might not escape a lynching.'

'You are trying to scare us off from doing this,' said one of men.

'I am telling you now what I have said all along,' said Turner. 'I think the whole idea is madness and likely to upset the apple cart. I am only taking part to ensure that you fools do not screw up everything that I have worked for here.'

Ike Holbeech tried to calm things

down a little by asking, 'What excuse can we have for all riding out together?'

'I do not yet know. Something to do with the miners would be my guess. If I can get them stirred up, then we will have good reason to go out to the diggings tomorrow morning. It would be no bad thing if we were able to lay the robbery of the stagecoach at their door as well, but this might take some serious thinking.'

'Ike says that you want to kill everybody on the stage. Is that so?'

'Yes it is so. I am not going to risk my neck on this. Even if we have scarfs round our faces and suchlike, it is still possible that something will give us away. I do not want one single witness tomorrow.'

'It seems hard,' said another man, 'if, as it might be, a woman and her child are travelling to Salt Lake City. Is there no other way?'

Turner eyed the man contemptuously. 'It strikes me,' he said, 'that you are in the wrong line of work. Instead of being a road agent, perhaps you would like to train as a Sunday School superintendent? That would be more in keeping with such a delicate nature. What the hell is wrong with you men? You want to rob a stage without bloodshed? You are a bunch of old women.'

In the end Ned Turner carried it his own way, as he always did. It was agreed that anybody in or around the stage would be killed and there was an end to it.

* * *

It was all well and good for Ned Turner to talk of getting the miners all stirred up but, had he but known it, he had already achieved this end by the massacre which he had initiated a day or two earlier. The two survivors of that incident had carried back reports of what had happened and there was not inconsiderable anger out at the diggings about what was seen as being cold-blooded murder. Those who had viewed the affair from inside the saloon might have been confused about the nature of that first shot, but this was not at all the case with the two men who had actually been standing out in the road. They were both adamant that the first shot had been fired from high overhead and that it was this which had broken the window in the saloon and given the sheriff and his friends the excuse to start firing. They had, in effect, walked into a trap.

Now nobody wanted to sour relations with the town as a whole, but at the same time some of the men at the diggings expressed the view most forcefully that they were damned if they were about to let anybody kill their companions in this way for no reason at all.

Some felt that they should avoid visiting Coopers Creek for a while, until things had calmed down somewhat. Others thought that this was precisely the right time to ride into town, to see what the devil was going on. Nobody denied that some of their number had made nuisances of themselves over the last few months, but nothing could excuse the murder of five people in this way.

It was decided that the arrival of a body of armed men might start another shooting match, which might not be needed. Twenty of the men agreed that they would enter the town in ones and twos towards dusk and see if they could not find a way to deal with this problem.

* * *

Nobody from Coopers Creek would have recognized their meek little baker, had they been up in the hills surrounding the town that morning. Jack Crawley had loaded his piece at the store and fitted caps on the nipples of the cylinder. The storekeeper had marvelled to see the deft and capable way in which Crawley had stripped and loaded his weapon. He later remarked to a friend that if you had not known Jack Crawley right well, you would have thought that he was a natural-born gunman, the efficient way that he handled that big old pistol.

Crawley had ridden a couple of miles from town, in the opposite direction from the diggings. He did not suppose that it would be the smart move to start discharging firearms around there, just at the moment. He had brought with him his holster and a belt. He took off his coat and he buckled the holster and belt around his waist. He would not be making any lightning draws from this rig, but it kept his pistol nicely to hand and he could pull it quicker than 'most anybody apart from a professional gun-fighter. The question to address now was, had he lost his eye?

Measuring out by pacing a distance of fifty feet from a slender silver birch, Crawley took his gun slowly from the holster. The trunk of the tree was about two feet wide: something like the width of a man's chest. He cocked his piece and then breathed in and out a few times to relax. Then, without aiming particularly, he brought the weapon up and fired. He could see at once that he had drilled a hole in the birch tree. He fired again, this time taking careful and steady aim. His second shot keyholed the first. He loosed off two more shots at the tree and then strolled over to look at the results.

The four shots were all in a space which could be covered by his hand. Two were overlapping and the others were no more than an inch and a half away from the first two. If he had been shooting at a man, it was a fair guess that all four bullets would have hit the heart. Although he knew that he had always been a fine shot, Crawley was still a little staggered that after a decade without touching any firearm he could still shoot so well.

Crawley spent an hour shooting and reloading. He was a little rusty on reloading fast and he suspected that this skill might be needed if things turned as rough as he expected in the next day or two. His was a cap-and-ball pistol, which meant that it did not fire cartridges, but needed to have powder poured into the chambers each time it was reloaded and a copper percussion cap affixed over each of the six nipples. The Colt Walker took twice the charge of any other handgun at that time and kicked like a mule.

One thing the baker did notice was that his holster flapped around in a most annoying fashion when he moved fast. Such an outfit might answer on the parade ground or while standing to attention besides a field gun, but it would not do for the sort of lively action which he might be getting up to in the near future. If he had to throw himself to the ground in a hurry, it was no good if his holster flipped up and his pistol fell out. There was a leather strap to hold it in, guarding against that very eventuality, but he wanted to be able to draw in a hurry if need be.

Before returning to town Crawley took from his saddle belt a knife and cut off the strap which held the pistol in the holster. He then ferreted around and found a long, rawhide bootlace. After cutting a small hole in the side of the holster lying on his thigh, he was able to thread the bootlace through the lower part of the holster and then tie it round his thigh. This prevented it from flapping round.

He looked down at the whole outfit and, despite the seriousness of the situation, laughed outright.

'I look like a regular gunfighter!' Crawley said out loud, shaking his head in disbelief.

It has to be said that Jack Crawley now cut a very different figure from that with which Coopers Creek was familiar. It was not just the pistol at his hip, but rather his entire demeanour, which had changed. It was almost as though the years had slipped away and that being a baker had been something at which he had only been playing. One gained the distinct impression when looking at him that this was the real Jack Crawley: an exceedingly strong individual who would brook no nonsense from others and was quite willing, if need arose, to back up his views and opinions with lethal force. It was a thoughtful and more than a little melancholy man who rode back into town after his target practice.

The first person whom Crawley met when once he had returned to town was a fellow member of the church. This man, no more than a casual acquaintance, was astounded at the difference which he noted in the mild-mannered fellow who often carried round the plate on Sunday services. Indeed, he barely recognized the baker in the man who walked towards him with his shoulders held back like a soldier and an air of deadly competence.

'Mr Crawley! I scarcely knew that it was you. You look somehow different, if you'll forgive my remarking upon it.'

'Good day to you, Mr Johnson. Yes it's me all right. I have just been for a ride up into the hills and I think that the fresh air has done me a power of good.'

Johnson noted with surprise that Crawley was carrying a weapon.

'I mind that this is the first time ever I saw you with a gun. You have left it a mite late, you know. After tomorrow, we will none of us be allowed to wear such things out and about, at least for some space of time. Until, that is, the present troubles have been resolved.'

Jack Crawley chuckled boyishly. 'I don't think so, Mr Johnson. I have a strong feeling that that particular regulation will not, as one might say, 'take'.'

'Well you surprise me, sir. You have always struck me as a law-abiding and peaceful man. I hope that you won't be setting a bad example by flouting the law at this stage in your life?'

Crawley laughed again, this time long and loud, as though he were at a theatre or something. In any other man Johnson would have suspected at this point that Crawley had spent a few hours in the saloon. The two of them parted amiably, but with Johnson scratching his head in a puzzled fashion and glancing backwards from time to time, as though he could not at all figure the play.

6

Ned Turner and his deputies had decided to ride out to the diggings that day and see if they could provoke some sort of incident. This would serve two purposes. First off, it would increase the feeling in the town that there was some kind of emergency. This was vital if the new regulation which Turner had made about carrying weapons was to be obeyed promptly on 26 October. As long as he could persuade the town that there was a danger of armed conflict, this would provide justification for banning anybody other than peace officers from carrying.

The second reason that Turner and his boys needed to cause trouble with the miners was that they would need a convincing excuse to go galloping off the following morning to rob the stage. If they could represent themselves as having been fighting to protect the town from more trouble, then it would give them an alibi for not having been in Coopers Creek at the very moment when the stage was hit. It might even prove possible, or so Turner thought, to implicate some prospectors or miners in the robbery.

Turner and Holbeech were walking along the street, heading over to the livery stable to meet up with the other five men, when they encountered Jack Crawley. Like Johnson from the church, at first they hardly knew that the man striding towards them really was the town's baker. 'What the hell,' said Ike Holbeech. 'Surely that is not the little baker that you have had the run-ins with?'

Turner narrowed his eyes at the sight of Jack Crawley walking along down the middle of the road like he owned the town. There was about the little man an air of, not precisely recklessness, but certainly confidence, like he was not afeared of anything or anybody. And of course, he was carrying a gun. This was a thing which, like everybody else in the town, Ned Turner had never seen before. It was not in the nature of a pleasant novelty for the sheriff.

When a half-dozen men attempt to impose their will upon an entire town, as Turner and his gang were doing right then, the whole enterprise is by way of being like a bluff in a game of poker. If all the other folk in town rise up and fetch their guns, then of course the half-dozen scoundrels will be run out of town. This was just the very thing that had occurred in Redemption. What you must aim to do is prevent folks from realizing their power and keep them cowed, so that they will not even dream of combining together and opposing your interests.

The sight of the town baker, of all unlikely people, walking along armed and with his head held high like he was a man of consequence was irksome in the extreme to Ned Turner. That sort of thing can be catching. One day it is just one man ignoring your rightful authority and the next, a heap of other citizens will be behaving in the self-same way. Before you know it, you have lost respect and people are questioning everything you say. Turner felt that this should be nipped in the bud right now. He headed straight for Jack Crawley, intending to put that man in his rightful place.

Crawley saw Ned Turner and his sidekick move off the sidewalk and head in his direction. If this was to be the confrontation, then so be it. He stood relaxed and easy, with his hand held just above his holster. As the two men approached, he stared straight at them, switching from one to the other, trying to gauge if either were about to draw.

Turner was shocked to see the baker just standing there, his hand obviously ready to go for his pistol. The last thing he wanted was to kill someone from the town like this, especially at such a tricky juncture. He stopped some twenty or thirty feet from Crawley. He had hoped to bully the man into surrendering his weapon, thus underlining his power and authority, but there is nothing lends a man less dignity than giving an order that is not obeyed. Looking at Jack Crawley now, it seemed unlikely to Turner that he would be following any instruction to give up his gun and so there was little point in even asking.

The little tableau in the public road was starting to draw attention from passers by, who were stopping to see what was what. It was certainly an uncommon scene, with the town baker standing face to face with the sheriff and his deputy. There might have been something a little comic about the set-up, except for the fact that Crawley had that quiet confidence about him of a man who is not under any circumstances or conditions going to back down. The longer the three of them stood there, the more it must have looked to the citizens of Coopers Creek as though gunplay was about to break out on the streets. Turner tried to defuse the stand-off.

'Jack, it is good to see you.'

Crawley said nothing at all, nor did he relax or move his hand from where it was hovering over the hilts of his pistol. Turner tried to ridicule the man into retreating.

'Jack, you are standing there like some gunman. What ails you, man? I will allow that we have had our differences lately, but this is unlooked for. Take your hand away from that pistol, you are making me nervous.'

'I am not threatening you, Turner,' said Crawley. 'I am just standing in the highway chatting to the local sheriff in a good-hearted manner. Unless, that is, you are wanting to make this into some sort of quarrel?'

'Quarrel?' said Turner, in apparent amazement. 'Who is talking of quarrels? I just came over to say hidy and you stand there like you are about to draw down on me.'

'I am not going to take out my

weapon, Turner. What gives you that notion?'

A thing that Ned Turner noted later and remarked upon especially was that Crawley did not seem to be angry, scared or blustering, which is the way that men almost always are in such cases. Instead, he gave the impression of a fellow who was having a good time. He was not actually smiling, but there was definitely a glint of amusement in his eyes. You would not have guessed in a thousand years that this cool and collected man was in reality none other than timid Jack Crawley, the baker.

'Hell's afire, Jack, we don't need to fall out over this. I have business to be attending to and I guess that your bakery does not run itself.'

'Don't you set mind to my business. I need no advice from you, Ned Turner.'

'Well then,' said Turner in friendly enough fashion, although he was seething with rage within, 'I suppose we may part friends? Do not forget though that as from tomorrow you will not be able to carry that gun in public as you are now doing.'

At this, Crawley smiled. 'Meaning, I take it, that if you encounter me tomorrow and I have this pistol with me, you will attempt to disarm me? That is what I would describe as a rash action. Let us hope that it does not come to that point.'

Turner and his deputy headed back to the sidewalk. There was quite a bunch of people standing there who had watched this whole episode and seen the sheriff's authority set at nought in the most humiliating way. They watched Turner curiously as he passed by and it seemed to him that they were less respectful than had been the case before. This he laid at the door of Jack Crawley and he determined then that there would be a reckoning for this at some later date when it could be undertaken privately.

As the two men walked to the livery stable, Holbeech enquired, 'You just going to let him get away with sassing you in that wise? I am surprised at that. I hope that you are not going soft.'

'Don't be a fool. I could hardly shoot him down in broad daylight. Fighting at night with a crew of drunken miners is one thing, gunning down the baker is something else entirely.'

'Well, he was armed,' Holbeech pointed out.

'So are half the men in this town. It was just funny seeing Jack Crawley with a gun; he wasn't threatening us or nothing. I shall deal with him in the future, don't you fret about that.'

'Still — ' began Holbeech, but Turner rounded on him savagely.

'You gossip like an old woman sometimes, Ike; you know that? I told you, I am going to deal with that man later. Just concentrate your mind on the matter in hand, which is finding some reason why we should ride out to the diggings tomorrow. I tell you now, that if we do not play this right, it is going to look mighty suspicious. The seven of us go off on some jaunt and then while we are away, the stage to Salt Lake City is robbed and everybody on board is killed. We must make this look convincing or else we are likely to find ourselves on the run again.'

* * *

Over at the diggings it had been decided that the most sensible course of action was to put together a deputation which would enter the town in a peaceable way and put the miners' grievance before those running Coopers Creek. It was not to be thought of that five men could be shot down in this way and that nobody was to answer for their deaths. It was clear that some accommodation would have to be reached and the only way to achieve that end was by talking.

Instead of their first idea of sending twenty men to enter the town in ones and twos, it was resolved that six men were to be chosen, who would ride to town that afternoon and lay their case before the citizens' committee.

At the same time as Ned Turner and his gang were saddling up in Coopers Creek, so too were the delegation of prospectors and miners who were about to start out in the opposite direction.

After his little run-in with Ned Turner, Crawley went straight over to Jim Kincaid's place. He stated the case plainly and forcefully.

'Jim, it is not altogether your fault, but your committee has landed us with a set of rascals who are looking to me as though they mean to prey on us. It is not to be borne and I want to hear what you have to say about it.'

'I don't know what I can tell you, Jack. Turner is not the man for the job that I hoped he would be and that's a fact. I do not see, though, that things are as bad as you are making them out to be.'

'The truth is that if we do not take action this very day, then by tomorrow it will be too late. Ned Turner and his bullies have it in mind that nobody but they will be bearing arms. Where will that leave the ordinary people here? Rouse up, man; it is for you to take a lead in this affair. When all's said and done, it was you and your friends who wanted a sheriff. It is for you to get rid of him.'

For a brief moment Jim Kincaid almost agreed to do the right thing. He knew very well that what Crawley was saying was no more than common sense. It was now a racing certainty that they had all been wrong about Turner and that he would cause only harm to the town. But despite this, Kincaid was aware of the $1,000 that he still owed Turner.

Worse still was where he had been helping himself to no small extent to the fines and taxes which Turner had been delivering to him. He was now in it up to his neck and there was not the shadow of a doubt that if Ned Turner went down, then he would drag Kincaid down with him. He would be finished in the town if once it was known that he had been stealing from them just the same as Turner.

'I can't help you, Jack. That's the long and the short of it. I wish I could, but I can't.'

'You say that I am wrong about Turner and his intentions?'

'No, I do not say that. I cannot help you. I am sorry.'

'I do not know,' said Crawley slowly, 'what part you have played in this mischief, nor yet what hold Turner has over you. But I tell you now that it will all come to light. You attend church, the same as me. You know what it says in scripture concerning the fact that what today we whisper in a darkened room will tomorrow be shouted from the very rooftops. Do not doubt that your secret will come out. The only course of action open to you now is joining with me in ridding the town of those men.'

'I'm sorry, Jack. Truly I am.'

'You won't help me, then?'

'I *can't* help you.'

It is surprising how quickly a rotten

apple can infect all the sound ones that surround it. One way and another, Ned Turner had managed to corrupt, compromise and threaten every one of the four members of the citizens' committee whom Crawley was able to track down that afternoon.

All this took up time and he decided to go back to his home to check that his family were all right. If only Coopers Creek were not such an isolated place. Crawley would have liked to send his wife and son out of town for a few days, until this whole business had been resolved. Seeing as that was not possible, the most he could do was check in on them regularly.

* * *

The seven men rode along at an easy trot. They were in no particular hurry to reach their destination as it was not too clear what they would be doing when they got there. The sheriff had voiced it abroad in Coopers Creek that he and his men were going to try and make peace with the men out at the diggings and hoped to smooth things over a little. This sounded awful thin, even to Turner as he related it, and he was not at all sure how things were going to pan out.

'What are we going to do tomorrow if the men in town appear with their guns as usual?' asked Ike Holbeech. 'If they just ignore your notices, then there will be too many of them to lock them all up in that old shed.'

'People are used to obeying rules,' said Turner. 'If you passed a law that nobody was to wear clothes in the street, trust me; most folk would step out of their houses buck naked. It is how people's minds work, at least in civilized countries. They will do as they are bid.'

One of the other deputies, a man whom Turner had known for some years, said, 'It will only need one or two people to ignore the new rule and others would follow. Are you sure that your precious town council are on your side as touching upon this? That Kincaid is not going to set out from his house carrying a piece, for example?'

Turner laughed. 'No, he is scared shitless. Do not set mind to that man. What you say has some sense in it. We must be sure to grab anybody whom we see with a gun at once, with no beating around the bush. This will show everybody that we mean business.'

Ike Holbeech announced suddenly, 'It sounds crazy, but I would say that if anybody is going to rock the boat, then it will be that little baker. He did not give me the feeling that he would be afraid to wear his gun tomorrow morning. He is a strange one; I cannot make him out at all.'

'He is nobody. Just a little man who is still vexed at me because it was me made sheriff and not him. He is of no account. I will settle with him in the next day or so, have no fear.'

'I am not so sure,' said Holbeech thoughtfully, whereupon Turner wheeled his horse round in front of Ike Holbeech, blocking his path.

'Who is the boss of this outfit, you or me?'

'Well now, you are the boss, Ned, as has never been in dispute. Howsoever, you are not a king nor anything like it,' said Holbeech mildly. 'Which is to say, that we can disagree with your reckoning of the state of play without your taking it as a personal affront, like.'

Turner was sobered. 'You do well to remind me of this, old friend,' he said softly. 'I was not aiming to buffalo either you or any of you others. Let us just say that Jack Crawley sticks under my skin like a cockle-burr. There will be a reckoning with that fellow, just mark my words.'

Turner's apologetic manner calmed down the situation and before they rode on the men fell to discussing their plans.

'What I would say is this,' said Turner. 'If we can stir up things at the diggings a little, then this would give us a pretext for returning tomorrow, on the grounds of completing our unfinished business.'

One of the deputies spoke. He was a quiet man, but something of a thinker.

'How does this strike everybody?' he enquired. 'Suppose that after we ambush that stage in the morning, we then race over to the miners' camp and shoot the place up a bit. This would go some way to backing up where we have been and what we have been doing at that time of day, when news reaches town of the stage being robbed.'

'That is a good scheme,' said Turner. 'I wish I had thought of it.' After the friction with Holbeech, he did not feel that there was any harm in buttering up all his men to any degree that seemed necessary. In fact, he had been about to suggest that very same thing, but was glad to be able to give the credit to another for the idea.

As they moved on towards the diggings Ned Turner brooded about what had happened in Redemption. This today was more or less a photographic image of that disastrous event. Then, just as now, his boys had been greedy for spoils and unwilling to take the long view. Turner was happy to find a good spot and then pick the bones of it clean over a protracted period of time, but Ike and the others wanted only to grab as much gold and cash money as they could lay their hands on, in the shortest possible space of time.

Left to himself, Turner would probably have given up road agent work entirely. After all, most of the gold being excavated in that section of Montana was already finding its way through Cooper Creek. It was simply a matter of creaming it off slowly and steadily. There was no need at all for waving guns around and killing folk.

* * *

Ned Turner was thinking in this gloomy and dispirited way at the same time as

Jack Crawley was having a pleasant meal with his family. Albert was thrilled beyond measure to see his father sporting a weapon for the first time that he could remember. He had never said anything to his father about it, but one or two boys at school had hinted that Albert Crawley's pa must be some sort of sissy, because he never yet was seen with a gun. Josie did her best to damp down the boy's enthusiasm, but she was fighting a losing battle and she knew it.

'Can I hold it?' asked Albert. Jack said:

'Yes, sure,' at precisely the same moment that his wife said:

'Nothing of the sort.'

'Please, Ma?' asked her son and Josie shrugged ungraciously. Albert took the pistol in his hands reverently and read with amazement the inscription around the cylinder. 'The hero of Buena Vista?' he said, stunned. 'Was that really you, Pa?'

'Well, it has my name there if you look,' said Crawley, by no means displeased at his son's reaction to the pistol.

'Why does it call you that?' asked Albert. 'I mean, why does it say 'hero'?'

'It means that your father was better at killing men than anybody else on the field that day,' said Josie tartly. 'It is nothing much to be proud of, being able to kill many men in that wise.'

Crawley laughed good-naturedly. 'There is somewhat in that, son. And your mother sets out the case honestly. They thought that I was a hero because I did not budge from one little hill and killed anybody who tried to get past me.'

'It's awful heavy,' said Albert. 'Are all pistols this heavy?'

'I wish you'd take that thing away from the child,' said Josie. 'He will pull the trigger directly and then we shall all be sorry.'

'It does not signify if he pulls the trigger,' said Crawley. 'That is a single action weapon. You must needs first cock the piece and then pull the trigger to fire it. It is not double action like some of the newer pistols one sees.'

'Will you show me how to shoot?' said Albert, his eyes shining with pride at seeing his father described as a hero.

'No,' said Josie, 'He will not and there is an end to the question. I never heard of such foolishness in all my born days.'

Albert looked at his father, who winked.

After his wife had set the table, Albert and his father sat down. This evening, Crawley himself wished to ask a blessing on the food.

'Lord, thank you for giving us food to eat when so many are hungry. Please watch over and protect this family and see that no harm befalls them. Amen.'

'Amen,' said his wife. 'Although if you are serious about wanting no harm to befall us, you might perhaps consider putting that dreadful thing back in the attic and going back to baking bread. Those apprentices of yours make the worst loaves I ever yet encountered. You are neglecting your business in order to march up and down the highroad like a bantam cock.'

'Josie, I am simply looking to the interest not only of others, but also of you and Albert. I cannot allow a set of villains to take over the town, it is not to be considered for a moment.'

'There are others in the town besides you, Jack; you are taking a good deal upon your own shoulders.'

'I will not stand aside and watch this town be robbed. I would not be the man you married if I was to behave so.'

'Will you put up that weapon if once you succeed in this endeavour?'

'What? You mean will I stop wearing my gun? Of course. It would get in the way no end when I was working. Besides which, there will be no need for it if we can run those boys out of town.'

'You promise?'

'Lord, Josie, but you are a strange one. You think I am glad to carry a gun again?'

'I think,' said his wife, 'that there is a

part of you which is glad. You look different since you took down that gun. You look different, walk different and act different. I would sooner be a baker's wife than married to a gun-slinger.'

Jack Crawley looked serious. 'There is something in what you say. You may have my word on this. I have done with ordering men around and taking responsibility for others. If we can settle this affair, then I shall take off this gun and there will be an end to it.'

Albert was dismayed. 'But Pa, you don't mean that you will put it away so that I do not see it again?'

'A gun is nothing wonderful, son,' said Crawley. 'It is like your mother says, being able to kill a lot of folks is nothing much to be proud of. There is more to being a hero than firing grapeshot for half a day. That is all nonsense what they wrote on this pistol. I am no hero.'

7

The six men from the miners' camps were proceeding down the road quietly, talking to each other in low voices. They had agreed one to another that perhaps their behaviour in Coopers Creek had been a mite troublesome to respectable people. They were determined to apologize for it and try to establish good relations again with those living in Coopers Creek. They were not bad fellows when sober, and even when drunk they generally caused more harm to each other than they did to people living in the town. What they purposed now was to make peace and see if it was not possible to have a truce.

Ned Turner and his gang were passing through a little wood of pine trees when they saw coming over the ridge about half a mile ahead of them a party of men from the diggings. Turner told his men to hold fast and they stopped dead, just inside the wood. This could hardly have worked out better if he had planned it for weeks beforehand, thought Ned Turner to himself.

'Listen, you men,' Turner said. 'Get ready to fire on these men. It is no matter whether or not any of them are shot, just make it known to them that we are pissed at them and that they had best not come on any further.'

'Why so?' asked Holbeech.

It was on the tip of Turner's tongue to tell his sidekick to mind his own damned business and just do as he was bid but, after the exchange earlier, he thought that it might be wiser to be more amenable to engage in reason and explanation.

'Well now, Ike,' he said, 'It stands to reason that we do not want any groups of those men clearing up misunderstandings, such as over the shooting the other night. I would be sorry for anybody in town to gain the impression that it was not those boys who started shooting and that we had men up on the roof with rifles.'

Holbeech nodded. 'This is true,' he said.

* * *

As they came nigh to the wood a sharp-eyed prospector observed that there was a party of riders blocking the path to town. He drew the attention of his fellows to this and they reined in their horses, uneasily aware that they were in a powerful exposed position if the intentions of those ahead turned out to be hostile. A couple of them loosened their rifles from the scabbards alongside their saddles.

'They seen us,' said Ike Holbeech, 'What now?'

'I do not want a bloody gun battle,' said Turner. 'All we require is some slight exchange of fire which will give us a reason for going back to the diggings tomorrow to arrest a couple of evildoers.'

Once again Turner's carefully planned schemes were wrecked by the impetuosity of his companions. As he was talking to Holbeech, one of the other deputies raised his rifle and fired towards the men in front of them. The shot went wide of the mark, but a grizzled mountain man who had in his time shot practically every creature that walked or crawled upon the face of the earth, swiftly pulled his hunting rifle from its scabbard, took careful aim and almost blew the head off the rider nearest to Turner and Holbeech. The ounce of lead caught the man in the eye socket and then pierced through his skull, tearing half his head away in the process. Blood and brain tissue sprayed into Turner's face and he began frantically wiping it away in disgust. The other group of riders had by this time turned tail, heading back the way that they had come.

There was nothing at all to be done

for the shot man, who must have died instantly. The others were all for riding after the miners and killing them all, but Turner reasoned the case out to them, explaining that they now had a perfect excuse to be going after the gunman the next day. It was a tragedy to be sure and they had lost a good friend, but at the same time, they could be sure to inflame passions in the town with this latest evidence of the dangers facing them. All in all, this would be likely to work to their advantage.

* * *

There was a subdued and uncertain atmosphere in the Tanglefoot as darkness fell. The place was very quiet and the owner was expressing himself strongly to anybody who would listen, to the effect that this present trouble was having a ruinous effect upon his trade. The man who owned the general store had said much the same thing at lunchtime. There was less fighting and drunkenness, it was true, but there was also a good deal less money flowing into the town.

At a table by the window were four older men and as they mulled over the state of things, it became clear that, like many in the town, they were having doubts about Ned Turner's way of going about his job.

'See now,' said one of the men, 'I do not say that we have not had difficulties here from men drinking too much and causing trouble. Nobody can deny that. But what you have to remember is that those same men are bringing their gold into town and spreading it around pretty liberally. I am thinking that it might be worth putting up with some inconvenience for the sake of that.'

'That is a good point, Bob,' said another, older, man. 'Ned Turner has certainly quietened things down, but it has made the prospectors stay away from town entirely. Look around you now and you will see that this place is half empty.'

'Then again,' said a third man, 'There is this business of making us not carry our guns. I do not altogether care for the look of some of those deputies that Turner has engaged. For all that Jim Kincaid says that they are doing us a favour, I have my doubts about some of those boys. Where will it leave us if only they are carrying?'

'I am starting to wonder if we might not have taken a wrong turning somewhere along the road. You say what you will about Jack Crawley, but I cannot imagine him bringing a lot of strangers into town and then passing a law saying that they could carry guns and we could not.'

There were nods and grunts of agreement to this. Whereupon, just as though they were acting in a play on a stage, Crawley himself entered the saloon, which was not a common occurrence. The men called him over.

When he had got himself a glass of soda the four men made room for Crawley. They all noticed that he was wearing a gun, which caused them to exchange glances and raise eyebrows questioningly. Bob Hargrave asked the question that they were all wanting an answer to.

'What's to do, Crawley? Why have you taken to wearing a gun?'

Crawley looked round the table and then said bluntly, 'I have put on a gun because I think that I am going to need it soon.'

The quiet and matter-of-fact way that he said this sent a chill round the men at the table. They knew Jack Crawley to be the most peace-loving and affable man in creation; always fooling round with church matters and helping out in the Sunday School. That he should strap on a gun and talk in that casual way of needing it, was alarming.

'Are you studying then to disobey this new rule that Turner has made, that which touches upon the carrying of firearms?'

'I reckon that I am,' said Crawley.

'And if you men had the sense that the good Lord gave a goat, you would all do the very same thing.'

'Mind,' said one of the men, 'you can see that it would be a good thing if there were no guns at all in a town.'

Crawley said, 'It is unconstitutional. Have you men not heard of the second amendment?'

'I don't rightly recall the precise words, but is that not something relating to the right to bear arms?'

'That it is,' said Crawley.

'Tell me,' said Hargrave, 'what does it say?'

'It says, 'the right of the people to keep and bear arms shall not be infringed',' Crawley told him. 'This sheriff of yours is violating the constitution of the United States and you men may be content to let him do so, but I for my part, am not.'

'When you put it in that way, I see what you are driving at,' one of the men said. 'I did not view it in that light before, but I see where this man, who was until a few weeks ago running the faro table, is getting a mite above himself to set aside the constitution.'

Crawley looked round the table, making eye contact with them all and then asked, 'Are you men ready to defy this ordinance?'

There is no telling how matters might have developed if Jack Crawley had been able to continue in this wise without interruption. He could be a very persuasive fellow when talking about something of this nature, which was close to his heart. In the event, there was a sudden flurry of shouting and swearing from out in the street, which was preceded by the thunder of hoofs as a party of men rode hard and fast up to the very door of the Tanglefoot.

Ned Turner burst in from the street, his face flushed and angry.

'Come see what those cowardly assassins have done now,' he cried. 'See how they have murdered one of your deputies.'

The corpse of the man who had been shot up in the pine wood was carried into the saloon by three men and then laid on a table, like it was on display. The thing presented a truly ghastly aspect. One eye had been blown out by the bullet, half the head was missing on that side, exposing the brain, and the other eye was wide open and staring sightlessly up at the ceiling.

'You all gather round,' said Turner harshly. 'Come close and see what those devils have done to this man, whose only intention was to uphold the law.'

One of the deputies who had brought the dead man in and laid him on the table, choked at this point when hearing this well known road agent lauded as one who upheld the law. Still, it looked as though Ned Turner knew what he was about, as indeed he did. The sight of the corpse's mutilated head was enough to put any normal person off firearms for the rest of his natural life.

Turner climbed on to a table and

called for the attention of those in the bar-room.

'I have some few words to say to you all,' he announced. 'This here is the result of people discharging firearms at each other. I aim to put an end to such practices and if that means nobody being allowed to carry guns for a while, well then, I reckon that that is fair enough.

'Now you all know that from tomorrow morning there will be no more guns carried by private citizens. Only duly appointed peace officers, which is to say me and my deputies, will be carrying. I hope that you all mark this.

'I am here to tell you now that I shall be right firm about this. Me and my men will be leaving town early in the morning to hunt down the villains who did this here to my man. When we return I do not want to see a single gun on the streets of this town.

'I think that you will own that under the peculiar circumstances in which we find ourselves, this is only common sense. Thank you for your time.'

Having delivered himself of these elevating sentiments, Turner went upstairs to his rooms, taking four of his deputies with him and leaving Ike Holbeech and the dead man behind.

Holbeech was in the mood to throw his weight around a little and, noticing Jack Crawley in the place, he went over to see if he could find some pretext for trouble. When Crawley saw Holbeech heading towards him, he stood out and moved clear of the table, standing in that same easy and relaxed way that he had shown when Turner and Holbeech accosted him in the street earlier that day.

'I will be marking you in particular, Crawley, tomorrow,' Holbeech told him, 'Checking, that is to say, that you are not carrying that piece on the public highway.'

'I shall welcome your attention,' said Crawley.

'I tell you now, once for all, if you set

a foot in the street with that thing on your hip, I shall be glad of the chance to knock you down, take your gun and chuck you in the lock-up for a day or two.'

Jack Crawley stood there calmly, looking like a man who was carefully mulling over some puzzle. At last, he said, 'If you feel that you are the man to take my gun from me, then you need not wait until the morning to make the attempt. Would you care to try your luck right now?' He said this in a friendly way, as though he were inviting Ike Holbeech to play a hand of cards with him.

There was some fidgeting, shuffling and rustling as those directly behind Crawley and Holbeech moved to one side.

'I am not authorized to take that action yet,' said Holbeech. 'But do not imagine that you may twist my tail without any fear. You would do well to back off. I am a bad man to get crosswise to, if you take my meaning.'

'Well,' said Crawley, 'if you are not about to do anything now, then I guess that I shall be leaving. I hope that we shall meet tomorrow.'

There was a sigh of relief when Jack Crawley left the saloon. It was the general view that they had come within a whisker of witnessing some sort of gunfight. That it had been the baker provoking Turner's right-hand man was little short of astonishing. Folk said to each other that it only went to show that you never could tell about men.

Once he was out in the street Crawley turned round to face the door to the saloon, figuring that Holbeech might come out after him. But after a few seconds he thought it safe to turn his back on the place and continue on his way home. He was anxious about his son and wondering if he at least could not be hidden away for the next few days.

* * *

Almost as though she had been able to read her husband's mind, Josie had already sent Albert off to stay with a friend of theirs on the very edge of town. This woman, who had a son the same age as Albert, also feared that there would be some kind of bloody confrontation in the next day or so and was not planning to allow her boy out in public until things had been settled one way or the other. She was happy to have Albert for a while to keep her own son company and stop him getting restless from being cooped up in the house by himself.

When he heard this, Jack Crawley smiled.

'Seems to me,' he said, 'That when you have been married as long as we have, you neither of you need to put things into words overmuch. You both kind of know what the other would have done.'

His wife went up and put her arms around him. She said, 'I have been a little shrewish recently, for which I hope you will forgive me. I have been worried. I guess that I was thinking along the same lines as you, that if anybody wished to get at you, then the best way would be by harming me or Albert. Now he is hidden away and those scoundrels don't know where, I feel a mite less anxious.'

'There is now you to consider — ' began Crawley, but here his wife burst in with the greatest irascibility.

'Lord, don't you think to parcel me up and send me off somewhere out of harm's way, like I was a child. Don't even think on such an idea. I am your wife and what we face, we face together. If I were any sort of hand with a gun, I dare say that I would be strapping one on myself to stand by your side, for all that I hate the things. No, I shall be staying right here in our house and I do not wish to hear one more word on that subject.'

'What will I do with you?' asked Crawley. 'Did you not promise to love, honour and obey me? What if I tell you that you *must* quit the house and go into hiding?'

'Then you would be starting a war on two fronts, which, as a West Point graduate, would not perhaps strike you as a wise move. Meaning that you would find yourself in opposition both to Ned Turner and your own wife. Let us not talk further on this. I am staying put here and there is an end of it.'

'I am going to go out for a couple of hours. I do not like the thought of you staying here alone.'

'Where are you going now?' asked Josie. 'I suspect that you will have what one might call a difficult day tomorrow. Would it not make more sense to get to bed early and have a bright fresh start in the morning?'

'I will not be long. I just want to ride out to the diggings and get the take of the men there on this day's events and how they see things developing generally. If we are not careful, we shall find a posse of armed men riding into Coopers Creek from that direction, intent upon revenge. If so, then it might not be only Turner and his boys who get caught in the line of fire.'

Josie Crawley shook her head. 'It seems to me that you are behaving like you was voted to be sheriff and not Ned Turner. You will wear yourself out in defence of this town and nobody will thank you. Still, I reckon that I knew what kind of man you were when I married you. I cannot complain at this stage of the proceedings and claim to have bought a cat in a sack. If you didn't carry on so, I would think there was something wrong with you.'

'Lock the doors and windows behind me when I am gone. I don't think that any of those rogues will try anything tonight. If they do, just tell them that I am out and you don't know where I am or when I shall return.'

* * *

Over at Turner's place above the saloon, he and his men were discussing the plans for the following day. Discussing would perhaps be putting the case too midly; they were quarrelling about it, with Ned Turner on one side of the fence and his deputies on the other.

'Is there nothing I can say to you men to cause you to reconsider on this matter of robbing the stage?' said Turner. 'After what has now happened, you must see that it is purely an act of madness to take out a coach so near to the town. Can we not at the very least put this off until next week, when a stage will be leaving from this very town? Another week would give us the chance to tighten our grip and make sure that people like Jack Crawley are out of the cart.'

In the eyes of his men Turner could see no encouragement for hoping that they would set aside this crazy scheme for a week. Four of the men had expressions of mulish obstinacy, while in Ike Holbeech's face he could see only cunning and crafty determination.

He might be wrong, but Turner was beginning to suspect that Holbeech had it in his mind to make a bid for leadership of the gang. It was at any rate Ike Holbeech who took it upon himself to speak for the other four.

'Fair's fair, Ned. All we are asking is for to get ourselves a little money. After that, we can allow things to quieten down for a spell. I do not see that we are queering things for your plans. There will be some slight ruckus, sure, but that will pass over soon enough. You are worrying too much. This is not the Ned Turner who I once knew. You used to be game for anything.'

Turner tried one last time to make his views plain and show the others how the land lay.

'Gold is coming into this town in a steady flow. There are more ways than one to skin a mule, and riding round like bandits is not the only road that will lead to us getting our hands on the stuff. Most of those men who dig up the gold no sooner have it in their hands than they fetch up in a nearby town and throw it away on gambling, drink or women.

'We do not need to seize that gold at the point of a gun. We can get the profits by levying taxes and fines; it amounts to the same thing in the long run. I will allow that it is slower than simply holding up a stage, as you men are set upon doing, but in the meantime we are comfortable here. We must play the long game.'

'Yes,' said one of the men. 'We play the long game while you are living here in luxury and we are lodged in poky little rooms. Share and share alike, Ned. We only want the same as you got, that is all.'

This was a long speech for this particular fellow; he seemed exhausted after making it and in need of refreshment from the whiskey bottle.

'Listen, Ned,' said Holbeech. 'We will rob this one stage and divide up the proceeds among us. There will be enough for all six of us to live very nicely until your own plans come to a head. Recollect that this stage will not even be passing through here. Ten to one, nobody in Coopers Creek will even hear about the robbery for weeks. You are worrying needlessly.'

'It will be like Redemption all over again,' said Turner flatly. 'That misfired because of this greedy haste for quick money, and we are going down the same road again. So be it. I see that you men will have your way. Do not blame me when a posse catches a-hold of you and hangs us all from the nearest tree.'

* * *

Jack Crawley approached the miners' camp with considerable misgivings, wondering if he would be fired upon before he even had a chance to open his mouth and explain his errand. He need not have fretted about that, because the first men he came upon recognized him at once as the town baker.

'Why, it's Mr Crawley, isn't it?' said

one. 'What brings you out here?'

'I need to speak to you boys, before things get altogether out of hand,' said Crawley. 'Do you have anything like a leader among you?'

One of the men laughed shortly. 'We do not go a whole lot upon leaders here,' he said. 'Speaking generally, we arrange things so that we are all in agreement.'

'That is what concerns me. Are you all in agreement now about descending upon Coopers Creek and creating hell?'

'Mr Crawley,' said the first man who had spoken to him, 'do you mind telling us what your interest in this is? We have no quarrel with you, nor anybody in the town except those damned villains who are running around with stars on their shirts.'

Crawley said, 'I do not want to carry on a long conversation, with me up here on my horse and you boys down there. Would you have any objection to me dismounting and perhaps having a cup of coffee with you all?'

The men looked at each other and gave almost imperceptible nods. 'I cannot see why not,' said one. 'Although I mind that matters have gone a mite too far for talking to be doing much to remedy things. Still and all, there is no harm in trying.'

In the normal way of things there was rivalry and sometimes ill-feeling between the prospectors, who were panning for 'placer' gold, and those who dug tunnels into the hillsides in search of it, but these two groups had evidently set aside their differences and had united in their anger about the events surrounding Ned Turner's election as sheriff.

'I will be the first to admit,' said one prospector, 'that our behaviour in town has not been like a party of schoolgirls on a Sunday School outing. I will also go so far as to say that we have been to blame for much of the trouble in the past. I hope that we can work something out in that direction. What is not to be borne is the killing of one of our number out of hand. We will be revenged for that.'

There were murmurs of assent when once this fellow had finished speaking.

'How if,' said Crawley, 'we in the town settle up with Turner and his men and bring them to justice for their crimes against your friends? Would that satisfy? I tell you straight, that if a crowd of you men ride into Coopers Creek as an armed band, it will unify the town behind Turner. You will do more harm than good.'

'That is fairly spoke,' said another of the men. 'But if you don't mind me mentioning it, Mr Crawley, you are only the baker and not a sheriff, nor even a deputy. How do we know that you can help bring this about?'

The men sitting on the ground around the fire nodded their heads and looked closely at the little man standing before them. It struck Crawley that they were probably as keen as he to avoid doing anything that could lead to something approaching a massacre. He could just imagine the townfolks taking up arms to repel what looked like an invasion. It did not bear thinking of.

'Matters are coming to a head one way or another tomorrow,' said Crawley. 'You can surely wait twenty four hours to see if I can bring this off? If I cannot, then you must do as you see fit.'

There was something about the baker that inspired confidence and trust. Even if he was mistaken in his estimation of things, nobody in that meeting doubted his sincerity and essential honesty.

'Would you like me to withdraw out of earshot while you talk this over?' asked the baker.

'No, I do not see need for that,' said a man. 'I do not think anybody here is keen to go shooting and killing if it can be avoided. There has been blood enough spilled. If you can put a stop to Turner, then we will come to town in a peaceable fashion and iron out our problems with the folk in Coopers Creek. The pity of it is that we did not do so before matters reached this point.'

Half an hour after this, Jack Crawley left the diggings with firm assurances that nobody would be taking any precipitate action for at least the next twenty-four hours. If things went right, he hoped that he would have sorted the town out before that time expired, and so averted what promised to be a most ugly battle which could not but result in a deal of bloodshed.

8

After the others had left Ned Turner got undressed and climbed into bed. He lay there in the darkness, trying to size up from every angle the scheme upon which he would be embarking in the morning. He still had no idea whether or not all the men in the town would voluntarily relinquish their right to bear arms. He had never got that far with his ideas in Redemption, although he had had it in mind as the next step; had things not gone sour so fast.

Turner had no intention of driving the miners and prospectors away from the town in the long term. When all was said and done he wanted their gold flowing into the town just as usual, but he also needed to ensure that it was coming into Cooper Creek on his terms and not anybody else's. He had installed his own man at the faro table and the next step would be to make a move on the saloon itself and bring that under his control. Then, little by little, he could begin to put the bite on the other businesses in the town.

Over the years Turner had observed, young as he was, that most people seek only a quiet and prosperous life for themselves and their families. They are not really bothered by abstract notions of justice and charity, so long as they have plenty on the table. By skimming just a reasonable amount off the top of all the town's financial dealings, Turner was sure that he could make the town thrive and still divert enough of the wealth in his direction to allow him to live very comfortably.

The fly in the ointment in this was that the members of the gang had correctly deduced that, from the way that the wind was blowing, they would be expected to live on a somewhat lower level than their boss; it was this that irked them. All those men really wanted was a bottle of whiskey, a pretty girl on their arm and enough cash to play poker. Which, of course, was why it looked to them to be a great idea just to knock over the occasional stagecoach when they were running short of money.

* * *

Wednesday, 26 October dawned bright and sunny, with not a cloud in the sky; a sky which was the colour of robins' eggs. Jack Crawley was up early and dressed neatly and quietly, so as not to disturb his wife. He put on not his ordinary working clothes, but what he called his Sunday-go-to-meeting outfit. This consisted of a black suit with a white shirt beneath it.

He shaved with special care that morning, not wanting to cut himself and so end up flecking blood on his best shirt. He smiled grimly as he took this precaution, reflecting that if things went badly for him that day, he would have more blood to worry about than a few specks of blood the size of pinheads dirtying up his collar.

He left Josie sleeping; there was little point in waking her just so she could fret about events over which she had no control. Crawley wanted to have a good breakfast and so he fried up a couple of eggs, having them with thick slices of bread and butter. He washed the meal down with several glasses of buttermilk and then brewed up some strong coffee.

While the coffee was brewing he lay a sheet of newspaper on the table to protect the cloth and laid his pistol upon it. He then hunted out an old rag and the can of oil. Using the haft of the butter knife, a proceeding which would have roused his wife to fury had she been around to see it, he tapped out the wedge that held the barrel to the frame of the gun. Then he slid the cylinder off the spindle and cleaned out all six chambers.

When the coffee was ready he poured himself a cup, with no milk and plenty of sugar. He wanted to make sure that he was on tip-top form that morning, and he had always found that a little extra sugar tended well to that end.

Between sips of coffee Crawley cleaned out the cylinder of his pistol thoroughly. He screwed up the rag into a point and twirled it round in each chamber, making sure that he removed every last trace of burnt powder. Then he oiled the spindle and threaded the cylinder back on to it, checking to see that it spun smoothly. After he was satisfied, he fixed the barrel back, tapping the wedge in lightly so that he could remove it easily should he need to do so.

The Colt Walker being a cap-and-ball pistol, he charged each chamber in turn with black powder and added a ball to each. As a precaution, he then smeared a little lard around in each chamber, just to be sure that a stray spark would not set off chambers other than the one he was actually firing.

Crawley gave the same methodical and careful attention to his old holster.

Although it was not a quick-draw rig, he made it a little smoother to pull from by smearing a film of lard on the inside, so that the pistol would slide out with less chance of sticking.

Once he had buckled on his belt and secured the holster round his thigh with the rawhide strip, he presented an appearance such as would make most men think twice before crossing him. Few who had not previously met him would have taken him to be a baker by trade; that much was certain.

* * *

Over at the Tanglefoot Ned Turner and his boys were also getting ready for action. They had breakfasted light and were now gearing up ready for battle. Like many men of their brand, they did not care to rely upon just one weapon, but bristled like hedgehogs with knives, guns and who knows what all else. One of the men had two guns, one at each hip, while another had one revolver and four throwing knives, with a muff pistol also concealed about his person.

Ned Turner only needed one pistol for most purposes, but today he decided to carry also the sawn-off twelve-gauge which he liked to use for close-up work. Most people knowing anything at all about firearms were inclined to do as they were bid when looking down the barrel of a twelve-gauge at close quarters. If push came to shove, it was a handy device for spraying mayhem around a scene should matters chance to come to shooting.

'I calculate that it is seven weeks since last we hit one of those stagecoaches,' said Turner quietly as they sat round a table in the saloon drinking coffee. 'Is that what you men also make it?'

Ike Holbeech nodded. 'Yes, I would say that that is about right. It was seven weeks ago, give or take a few days. Why?'

'Because I am thinking that perhaps they will not be so much on their guard today,' said Turner. 'Perhaps they will think that this band has broken up or moved on elsewhere.'

Before he was made sheriff, Ned Turner had gone out to meet up with his men every few weeks for various robberies; sometimes of stages and other times of individual travellers whom they had reason to suppose were carrying large sums of money or quantities of gold. One week the stage to Salt Lake City passed through Coopers Creek and the next it went through another small town to the south.

This day it was due to visit that other town and then pass a few miles south of Coopers Creek. Turner and his men would hit it five or six miles from town and then race across to the diggings and stir up a fight there.

'Everybody does know that we are supposed to be going over to the camp to try and arrest the man who killed our partner yesterday?' asked Turner of Holbeech.

'That is the story which is current, yes,' the other man replied.

'If, when we return to town, I see any man carrying a weapon, I intend to grab that man at once and lock him up. There is room for six or seven in that lockup, at a pinch, but I do not think it will come to that,' said Turner.

'What about your friend the baker?' enquired another man.

Turner glared at the fellow coldly. 'I shall be settling accounts with Jack Crawley as soon as we get back here. I want to do it quietly though, without overmuch fuss and bother.'

'Perhaps he will have already taken the hint and dug up,' suggested Holbeech. 'That would be a good thing indeed, if he had already fled when we went looking for him.'

Turner shook his head doubtfully. 'I do not see that happening. I will have to go head to head with that man before the sun goes down this day.'

* * *

Turner and his gang rode south out of town at around 6.45 that morning, before most folk were up and about. They saw one or two men, neither of whom was carrying.

'That is a good sign,' said Holbeech.

Half an hour later Turner and his boys were loitering in the trees lining the road that the stagecoach would be taking. The six of them were not bothering to conceal their faces, it being their intention to make sure that nobody was left alive to identify any of them.

* * *

Jim Kincaid was woken up early by a hammering on his front door. He couldn't for the life of him think what might be afoot and neither could his wife, who lay next to him in bed, looking scared.

'It's probably nothing at all,' said Kincaid, unconvincingly. 'All the same, I had best see what's what.' He pulled on his pants, tucking his nightshirt into them. He did not, at this moment, look much like the town's leading citizen. Shielding what he was doing with his body, so that his wife didn't see, he pulled open a drawer in the cabinet and reached out a small pistol.

'All right,' he bellowed down the stairs, 'I'm a coming.'

On the doorstep stood, as he half-guessed would be the case, Jack Crawley. Crawley looked nothing at all like any baker you ever heard of. He was dressed from head to toe in black and was sporting some big, heavy pistol.

'Jack, what the hell are you about, banging on my door at this time of day. You scared my wife out of her wits. Can this wait until a more respectable hour?'

Kincaid tried to keep things as light-hearted as he could manage, hoping against hope that if he joshed and talked lightly, then there wouldn't really be any sort of crisis to deal with. It was a forlorn enough hope, which

Crawley dashed to pieces when he said:
'It's life and death, Jim, as well you know. Let me in.'
'Well, if I must. Come into the kitchen. And keep your voice down, I don't want my wife to be alarmed.'
When the two men were in the kitchen with the door shut, Crawley said, 'This is where the knife meets the bone, Jim. That precious sheriff of yours has ridden off on the Lord knows what mischief this morning, and then when he returns, he is aiming to prevent every man in town from exercising his right to carry arms. You know it is wrong and it is for you to take a stand.'
Jim Kincaid looked frightened to death by the fix in which he found himself. He sat down at the table and sank his face into his hands. After a second or two he looked up and said,
'I can't do it, Jack. There's the truth of it. I just plain can't.'
There was no point that Crawley could see in urging this man to stiffen

his sinews and stand up to Turner and his bullies.

'I will do it,' said Crawley. 'I will do it, but I need some authority. You made Ned Turner sheriff; you must have the power to strip him of the job if need be?'

'Lord God, Jack, I durst not do that. There are reasons that you don't know.'

'I can guess,' said Jack Crawley grimly. 'And my guess would involve gambling debts and Turner advancing you credit.'

Kincaid looked up fearfully.

'That's nothing to the purpose though,' continued Crawley. 'I told you, I will do it my own self. You can swear me in as sheriff as you did with Turner. You have that authority?'

'I guess. I have not given it much thought.'

'You need not give mind to it now. Best you don't, all things considered, or you would like as not talk yourself out of the notion. Do you have another sheriff's badge?'

'Yes, I think so. This is madness. You are suggesting that I swear you in as sheriff and that you then go up against Turner and those five men of his? It will be plain murder, I won't have a hand in it.'

'I don't see that you have another choice, Jim. Truly I don't.'

'Wait here,' said Kincaid and left the room. He returned a few seconds later carrying a Bible, a piece of paper and a silver star. 'Repeat these words after me,' he said.

Having sworn to uphold the peace without fear or favour, Jack Crawley pinned the star on his jacket. As he was about to leave he turned and said to Kincaid, 'I do not know what part you have played in all this, Jim. I do not want to know and shall not enquire into the matter, either now or later. But if I can clear this up and run those rascals out of town, then I look for you to resign your position as head of that committee of yours. Is that fair and just, would you say?'

Kincaid nodded. It was better than he had expected or deserved. Jack Crawley was solid gold right through and why he had not backed him for sheriff in the first place was something of a mystery to him now.

Outside in the street Coopers Creek was gearing up for what most of the citizens assumed would be just another day. Outside the store the owner was sweeping the sidewalk; shutters were going up and people were getting ready for work. Crawley stopped the first man he met, a young fellow called Ted Baxter, who worked in the livery stable.

'I observe that you are not wearing a gun,' said Crawley.

'I don't often do so,' said the boy, who could not have been much above eighteen years of age.

'Today is a special occasion, son,' said Crawley. 'I have just been appointed sheriff of this town and I am urging all citizens to wear their guns pridefully as befits men who are not afraid of defending their freedom. Go home and get yours.'

'What of this new law?' said young Baxter. He indicated one of the bills which announced that from this day the wearing of guns was prohibited. Crawley reached up and ripped down the poster.

'What new law?' he asked.

For the next hour or so, Crawley walked round town, stopping every man he saw and telling him to go home and fetch his gun and to remember the second amendment. Folk said later that the way that baker talked about the case, you would think that men had some sort of duty to be armed that day.

* * *

While they waited for the stage Turner and Holbeech talked in a friendly enough way about what would need to be done in the coming weeks. They agreed that the first thing to do would be to encourage the men from the diggings to start drinking and gambling again in Coopers Creek, provided always that they left their guns at home.

'It is my belief,' said Turner, 'that they will forget about the unpleasantness of the last week or two and things will return to normal. People have short memories.'

'I believe that you are right,' said Holbeech. 'We have shown them who is in charge in the town and they are not apt to forget this in a hurry. It is a shame about Jed getting killed yesterday, but I do not think that that affects the lie of the land.'

'No,' said Turner, 'I am sure that we will reach an accommodation with them.'

'Hold up,' said Ike Holbeech. 'Look over yonder.'

The stage was heading towards them. There was no sign of any extra precautions, such as outriders or more guards than usual.

'I reckon,' said Ned Turner, 'that they thought the Turner gang had gone out of business. They have made what you might call an error of judgement there.'

From all that they could see there was just the driver and one man sitting next to him. They looked as relaxed and cheerful as could be.

Now the Turner gang had never been noted for the finesse of their operations. They relied upon overwhelming force and brute violence when it was called for. On this venture they did not propose to leave a single survivor and so had not even bothered to conceal their faces with handkerchiefs or anything of that nature.

As the stage came nigh to where they were waiting, Ned Turner cried, 'Let's get them, boys!' and the whole boiling of them galloped down the slope towards the coach. The blinds were down on the windows and so they could not see what sort of passengers it contained.

As he rode down to the road Turner shouted to the driver, 'Stand to and you will not be harmed!'

They did not want to kill the driver before the coach had stopped, chasing after and stopping a runaway coach being the devil's own work.

The driver reined in the horses and then turned and rapped smartly on the roof of the coach, whereupon the blinds flew up and Turner and his men received the greatest surprise that any of them had received in the whole course of their lives. Instead of the women and children that some of them had feared they might be compelled to kill were three men, each armed with the Smith & Wesson company's latest 'Volcanic' repeating rifles.

Instead of firing a shot and then fooling around with a flask of powder before they could fire again, the wielders of these weapons could shoot again and again without reloading, simply by jerking up and down a lever. This fed brass cartridges into the breech from a tubular magazine.

The explanation for this unexpected turn of events was a simple one. Sick to the back teeth of the raids on their coaches, the company had hired Pinkerton's Detective Agency to put an end to them and to protect their interests. Pinkerton's had suggested fitting one of the stagecoaches out as a decoy and then seeing if they might lure the bandits into attacking.

Ned Turner and his boys knew nothing of all this; all that they saw was that instead of being the ruthless predators that they had thought themselves to be, they had become the prey.

After bringing the coach to a halt and fixing the brakes so that the horses would not bolt, the driver and his mate jumped off their seats and over to the other side of the vehicle, so that they were not sitting targets for the six riders who were racing down upon them. They opened the door on the other side of the stage, reached out 'Volcanic' rifles themselves, and also commenced firing at the erstwhile bandits.

With five men armed with the most modern and up-to-date repeating rifles, the robbers didn't have a chance. The man next to Ike Holbeech went down almost at once with a bullet through his chest. Holbeech was firing with his pistol, but he did not know that steel plates had been fixed to the inside of the coach, meaning that most of his bullets were striking the bodywork of the stagecoach and just bouncing off harmlessly.

Two bullets hit Holbeech's horse and he was catapulted over its head as the creature skidded to a halt. Another rider jerked back convulsively as he was shot through the throat. The steady fire from the five repeating rifles made it sheer suicide to continue and Ned Turner brought his horse round, thinking only of escape.

* * *

Jack Crawley had had only limited success with encouraging the men he encountered to disregard Turner's new rule about guns. Fact was, some of those he spoke with thought that the little man had lost his mind and was now pretending to be the sheriff, when everybody knew that, for good or ill, that post was in reality held by Ned Turner. One or two of the younger men took him at his word, but by the time the town was up and doing that morning, only three men besides Crawley were armed. None of those others was more than twenty years old, and Crawley thought that Turner and his boys would make short work of them. It would be, as he had suspected all along, entirely down to him.

As Turner rode back to Coopers Creek, the full magnitude of the disaster began to sink in. He had lost absolutely everything. His men were killed, he had no back-up in town and precious little money now. As if that was not all bad enough, the men from the diggings would surely be seeking vengeance against him before long.

Things looked bleak as they could be and yet Ned Turner had never been a quitter. Would it still be possible to retrieve something from the ruin? The more he thought it over, the more possible it seemed to him.

He still had Jim Kincaid, Abe Calthorpe and a couple of other members of the town council in his pocket. That was a good beginning. Not to mention where he was still officially the sheriff of Coopers Creek. The more he turned matters round in his mind, the more he persuaded himself that all was not lost at all. It would just need some cold nerve and bluffing to bring the situation round to his advantage once more.

By the time that he was in sight of town Turner was feeling pretty confident of coming out on top once more. Surely there must be some likely young fellows in the town who would jump at the chance of being his deputies? Unprincipled young men who would be glad to make some easy money under his instruction. Men like that boy Ted Baxter, who worked over at the livery stable.

There was no time like the present and he decided to stop off at the livery stable before getting freshened up, and see if he could not offer the Baxter boy a job. It was not the first time that Ned Turner had apparently lost everything, but he had always bounced back again. There was no reason why this time it should be any different.

As he dismounted outside the livery stable Turner thought to himself that there was even a bright spot to the disaster. Ike Holbeech had been disposed to be a mite too contentious in recent times and it would be no bad thing to start over again with a new crowd entirely.

He received something of a shock when he entered the barn and discovered that Ted Baxter was strutting round the place as bold as you please, with his gun hanging at his hip. The sight of this put Turner out of countenance and, whereas before he had been minded to court Baxter and offer him a job, he now demanded an explanation for this flagrant disobedience of his orders for the town.

'Did you not see those notices which me and my men posted up around town?' asked Turner.

Baxter did not seem the least abashed, saying, 'Well, I reckon that those bills might not signify over-much now, Mr Turner.'

'We'll just see how much they signify. I came here to offer you a more important job than errand boy in this place, but now I am more than half minded to lock you up for a spell. What do you say to that?'

'I think,' said Ted Baxter, 'that things might have changed since you put up those bills, sir. We have a new sheriff.'

'New sheriff? What the hell are you talking about, you damned young fool?'

'There is no call to speak so. I only know what I have seen and that is that you are not the only person in this town with a sheriff's badge. Truth to tell, it is a little confusing and I am hoping that we can get to a point where there is only one such.'

'I tell you now, once and for all, there is only one sheriff in Coopers Creek and you would do well not to get crosswise to him. That is me. Who is this other sheriff of who you talk?'

'Why, it is Jack Crawley of course. He came by here earlier and told me that things have changed.'

'Changed, have they? We will see about that. Where is he?'

'I couldn't say. Did I understand you to say that you were a going to offer me a job?'

'Job, nothing. I will be back in short order to speak further and if you are wise, you will not be wearing that gun when I get back. I am going to settle this nonsense concerning a new sheriff first. I am leaving my horse outside for a space. Set mind that no harm befalls her.'

With that, Turner left the livery stable

in a bad frame of mind. He walked down the street to the saloon, intending to go to his rooms so that he could sit quietly and fathom out the best course of action.

Standing in the road ahead of him was a slim figure dressed in a black suit. This man too, just like Ted Baxter, was wearing a gun. It looked to Ned Turner as though the whole town was ignoring his instructions. He wondered what he was going to do about it now that he had nobody to assist him. Then, with a shock, he realized that he knew this black-clad man.

It was Jack Crawley.

9

Crawley was standing in the middle of the road as relaxed as could be, his hands hanging by his side, the right one just above the hilt of his pistol. Ned Turner stopped thirty feet from the baker.

'Well, Jack,' said Turner, 'what will you have? I am going up to my rooms. Will you hold the road against me?' He laughed as though the very idea was ridiculous.

'Where are your friends, Ned?' asked Crawley. 'I have business with them as well as you.'

'What business would that be?' enquired Turner, interested in spite of himself.

'The same business as I have with you. I am going to take their badges and tell them that they are no longer peace officers. Which I am also telling you. If you would take off that star and hand it to me, then we might be able to arrange this without unpleasantness.'

People passing by had stopped to watch the spectacle taking place in the main street of their town. Because the two men were some distance apart, they were compelled to raise their voices so as to be heard, and so everybody in the vicinity could hear what was being said and was tolerably sure that something would have to give. Apart from those hanging round on the sidewalk, there were a number of people peering out of windows to see what would happen next.

'Are you sure that you have not bit off more than you can chew comfortable, like?' asked Turner. 'There is still time to turn aside from this road. I don't want to hurt you, Jack.'

'Nobody will get hurt if you just hand me your badge and also your gun. Otherwise, I am sure I don't know what the outcome of this will be.'

'That's enough fooling. Move from

my way now or I shall settle with you. I am serious, Crawley. Just let this go.'

Jack Crawley tensed slightly, and whereas before, his hands had been hanging loose and relaxed by his side, he had now raised his right hand a fraction, so that it was poised over his pistol. Other than that, he gave no indication that he had heard what Turner had said. The tension was nigh on unbearable, like the feeling you sometimes get just before lightning strikes.

Turner's hand had closed over his pistol and it was halfway out of the holster when the bullet hit his wrist, shattering the bone. His left hand twisted round and he had begun scrabbling for the gun with that hand instead when Crawley's second bullet took him in the chest. He sank slowly to his knees, disbelief on his face. Then he fell sideways and sprawled in the dirt, his lifeblood pumping out into the roadway.

Jack Crawley turned to those standing and watching. 'I call upon you folk to witness that it need not have come to this,' he said. 'I gave him the chance to surrender peaceably and he chose to go for his gun. His blood is upon his own head.'

One of the men on the sidewalk said, 'It was not your fault. You gave him his chance . . . Sheriff.'

With the shooting over, people came hurrying out into the street to view the scene. The little baker stood there looking sadly down at the body of the man he had just killed. He could not yet afford to relax though, because he was wondering what had become of the other five men who had ridden out that morning.

'Does anybody know where that man who runs the faro table is staying?' asked Crawley of the gathering crowd. 'The fellow who took up after Turner here left off?'

Somebody gave him directions to the house where this person might be found and Crawley went there.

Seth Roebuck was an old acquaintance of Turner's, but his involvement with the man was limited to helping him fleece other card-players. He had arrived in Coopers Creek a few months after Ned Turner had established himself in the town, and from then on had held various piddling little jobs, interspersed with spells of running games in the saloon with Turner.

'I know Ike Holbeech, of course. Him and Ned were old friends from way back. As for those others, I couldn't tell you. I knew one or two of them by sight and I guessed that they were mixed up in Ned's other business.'

'What do you mean,' asked Crawley. 'What other business?'

Roebuck stirred uneasily. 'Oh, you know. The other tricks he was up to.'

'No,' said Jack Crawley patiently, 'I do not know. What were these other tricks that he was up to?'

'Well, I am meaning that I kind of thought that he and those boys were road agents from time to time. Holding up stages and suchlike. Mind, I do not know for sure, but that was what was said.'

'Do you have any notion at all where those other men might now be found? There is an urgency here which I would have you mark.'

'I do not know and that's God's honest truth. If you force me to guess, then I would say, now that he is dead as you tell me, that they were perhaps going to hit some coach or other. But that is only a guess.'

Crawley stared hard at Seth Roebuck for a few seconds, before saying, 'I have an idea that you know more about all this business than you are letting on, although I cannot prove it. I will tell you now, though, things are going to be changing round here in the near future. As you may have noticed, I am now the sheriff in this town and crooked card games will soon be a thing of the past here. Just recollect that, will you?'

It looked like everybody in town was crowded round the corpse of the man who had lately been their sheriff. Much as he had disliked Ned Turner, Crawley found something distasteful about the idea of his mortal remains being gawped at like they were a carnival sideshow. He went over to the people peering at the body and remarking upon the quantity of blood. He noted with disgust that women and children were among the sightseers.

'I want you all to move on now,' said Crawley. 'Have some reverence for death. You would not wish to think of your own relatives being stared at and remarked upon in this way after their deaths, now would you? I would have some respect now for this man. He has paid the price for his deeds and should now be left in peace. Move away now, I say.'

As the crowd began to disperse three men rode up. One of them announced, 'We are looking for the sheriff of this here town.'

A youth called out from the crowd:

'Well you can take your pick between the living one or the dead,' which provoked a few wry chuckles. Jack Crawley went up to the riders.

'I am the sheriff here. My name is Jack Crawley.'

One of the men peered closely at the sheriff, saying, 'Not Captain Crawley? Surely to God not 'Give 'em hell' Jack Crawley?'

'I was associated with that expression once upon a time,' he replied. 'But that is neither here nor there.'

'Is it not?' said the rider. 'Do you not remember me then? I was with you that very day, standing by your side. I am grieved to find that you have forgot your sergeant.'

Crawley gazed in astonishment upon a man he had not set eyes upon for over ten years.

'As I live and breathe, it is Sergeant Jackson! Now what in creation brings you here at such a time? I am not persuaded that it is chance alone.'

The three men dismounted and his former sergeant shook Jack Crawley warmly by the hand. He noticed the pistol with delight, exclaiming, 'Still wearing your farewell present too, sir. That is pleasing to see.'

Crawley laughed in an embarrassed way. 'I have not been in the custom of wearing it like this until recently. It is a long story. What of you? You are no longer a sergeant, I'll be bound.'

'No sir, I am not. I am an agent of Pinkerton's. The detective agency, you know. We have just had a little run-in not far from here and were pursuing a man. Who, if I am not mistook, is that very man who lies dead in the road there.'

'What was he doing that you should have been chasing him?'

'Attempting to rob a stagecoach. Only he got a little more than he bargained for, him and his friends — all of them.'

'Friends? How many would you say?'

'Five or six. Why, what is your connection with the affair, if you don't mind me asking?'

The curious crowd was beginning to

re-form around Crawley and the Pinkerton's men. Ned Turner's body had been forgotten in the excitement of seeing some Pinkerton's agents up close. Crawley selected a young lad and asked him, 'Do you know where Abe Calthorpe, the undertaker, has his premises?'

'Yes sir, I surely do,' replied the boy.

'Well, here's a dime. Run over there and tell Mr Calthorpe that I urgently require him to come over here and collect up this body. Be sure to tell him that it is urgent.'

The young man dashed off. Crawley turned back to the man who had once been his sergeant.

'Why don't we go over to the saloon and you can explain your part in this and I mine. I do not want to deliver a public lecture, which is what our conversation is becoming with all these folks clustered around us like we were some species of entertainment.'

He turned to the people gathered round them. 'Come now, I am sure that you folk have homes to go to and business to attend.'

Once he was settled comfortably in the Tanglefoot with the three Pinkerton's men, Crawley asked, 'So how did you come across the fellow now lying in yonder road?'

'It is no great mystery,' said Jackson. 'I guess that you people here know all about the raids on the stages to Salt Lake City. Just recently there was a real big attack, with people killed. The company hired us people to put a stop to it.'

'I take it then,' said Crawley, 'that Turner, the dead man, and his gang attacked a stage when you were near by?'

Jackson laughed roguishly. 'Well sir, there was no trusting to chance in that way. We were given the use of an old stagecoach, which we modified, as one might put it. We affixed metal plates on the inside, so that stray bullets could not penetrate the interior and also took out one seat and replaced it with a rack of repeating rifles. We stowed saddles and so on at the back, where the luggage is normally to be found, and harnessed up our own horses to pull the thing.'

Jack Crawley shook his head in admiration at the ingenuity of the men.

'And I suppose,' he said, 'that Turner and his boys just came riding down on you and you then opened fire?'

'That is just so, sir. All but he you call Turner was killed and he fled the scene. All that remained for us to do was unharness our horses and tack them up with our saddles and we were ready to go in pursuit.'

'Well, I suppose that that is the end of our adventure. Where are the bodies of the other men who were killed?'

'They are still out where the ambush took place. We left two of our number there to tidy up the place a bit. Besides which, you would not want to leave a coach full of modern rifles unattended for too long.'

'What are these famous rifles that you keep talking of? Might I see one?'

'Surely,' said Jackson. 'Davy, scoot out and fetch in one of those 'Volcanics'.'

When the man returned with the rifle, Crawley was surprised at the elegance of it.

'This holds the brass cartridges, I suppose?' he asked.

'That's it, sir. You just flip that lever after every shot and away you go. No fussing round with ramrods, caps, flasks of powder, wadding and all the rest of it.'

'Are they reliable? Meaning, do you get many misfires?'

'To speak truly,' said Jackson, 'You do. But that don't signify, because if it happens that you have a dud cartridge, you just work that lever to eject it and you are ready with a new one.'

'Well,' said the new sheriff, 'I am mighty obliged to you boys for what you have done this day. I reckon that you saved my own life. I was wondering how I was going to cope with facing six men, and all along you were shortening the odds in my favour without me knowing a thing about it. Thank you.'

'That is nothing, sir,' replied Jackson. 'It is just like old times. Don't you ever miss the army at all?'

'No. I never really liked killing men.'

'Tell me,' said Jackson. 'Do you want us to bring those bodies here, those of the men who attacked us? There is the matter of rewards, and if you are the sheriff here, we will need some document from you. After all, this could be a lot of smoke I am giving you. You have not actually seen any corpses, nor yet our credentials as Pinkerton's agents.'

'Yes, if you were to do so, that would be fine. What will you do, load them into your coach and bring them that way?'

'Yes, I reckon so.'

After parting from his old sergeant and promising that he would have the leisure to spare for a longer conversation at a later time, Jack Crawley thought that he had best go out to the diggings and let the boys out there know that they would have no call to come riding into Coopers Creek like a band of marauders, seeking vengeance against Turner and his crew. First though, he went over to his own home to let Josie know that the trouble was over now.

'Well,' said his wife, when he had filled her in upon the state of play, 'I will not say that I am sorry to see you safe and sound. I could have wished though that you had been able to achieve your end without snuffing out the life of a fellow being.'

'It is much on my own conscience, I do assure you,' Crawley told her. 'Howsoever, it is the fact that had I not defended myself as I did, then you would be grieving as a widow now and our son would be a fatherless orphan.'

'I mind that well enough,' said Josie, her tone softening. 'I was not berating you, just telling you of my sorrow. What's done is done. On which topic, I see where you have a star upon your jacket. Does that mean that you are to be sheriff after all?'

'I cannot say for certain yet. I must ride out to the diggings and tell the men there that there will be no need for further bloodshed. I had best do that at once. You can fetch Albert home now and tell everyone you meet that the trouble is ended.'

The two of them embraced and the sheriff made off towards the diggings. Meanwhile, the Pinkerton's men were riding back to where they had left their companions guarding the bodies of the outlaws.

As he trotted along the track leading to the mines and the prospectors' shacks, Crawley felt an overwhelming sense of relief. When he had climbed out of his bed that morning, he had no idea at all whether he would still be alive and breathing by the evening. Now, as far as he was able to gauge,

Turner and all his friends were dead and the peril had passed.

Being the sort of man he was, Jack Crawley was beginning to blame himself for the whole series of events which had begun just a few short weeks earlier. If he had been a little more forceful at the meeting which had elected Ned Turner, then perhaps he could have averted all these deaths. He had known even before he stood up to speak that evening that nobody was likely to vote him in on the facts as they were known. Should he have told those there of his strong suspicions, rather than limiting himself to what he knew to be true?

It was fruitless to speculate over how things might have turned out and so he began to think about more pleasant matters, such as the sudden and unexpected appearance of his old friend Jackson.

The men at the diggings were pleased to see him. When his star was spotted they came up to congratulate him.

'There will have to be changes,' Crawley told them. 'You know this as well as I do. Matters were getting out of hand to some great degree over the summer. Nobody in the town wants to see the level of violence such as they witnessed, even before Turner was voted in.'

'This is agreed between us already, Mr Crawley. It can be said that we ourselves were to blame for some of this. What me and a few others say is that it would be no bad thing if we could come into town and talk things over with your citizens' committee.'

'Yes,' said Crawley, 'I have been thinking along much the same lines. It is a shame that we none of us thought this way some little time before, but there it is.'

* * *

Now while Jack Crawley and the men at the diggings were congratulating themselves on the end of the troubles in which they had become embroiled, the Pinkerton's men were almost back at their decoy stagecoach.

They too were pleased at how neatly things had turned out. Jackson had been too modest to boast of it, but the whole plan of running dummy stages full of Pinkerton's agents along the Salt Lake City route had been his in the first place.

This day's sequence of events had proved that the project was a sound one and the killing of a whole band of robbers in this wise would do him no harm with his employers.

As the three of them came through the wood and into sight of the stage, something was puzzling Jackson; there was no sign of the two men he had left to tidy up the site of the abortive robbery.

'Hold up,' he said to his companions. 'Something is amiss here.'

They reined in their horses and surveyed the area at a distance. Nothing was moving at all and the bodies of the outlaws were still scattered around the coach.

'Where have those men got to?' Jackson wondered out loud. 'Hallo, there!' he called. There was no reponse.

Jackson drew his pistol and the two men on either side of him did the same. The three of them walked their horses down to the coach, where they dismounted and tried to make some sense of things. Of the two men who had been left behind there was no sign at all.

It was not until they looked a little closer at the bodies of the bandits that they began to have some notion of what had happened. As he turned over one of the men, Jackson gasped and said, 'Ah, shit!' The dead man was Mike Todd, one of those who had been riding the stage that day. The other man who had been left behind was also there and had also been shot dead.

Here is what had happened. During the ill-fated assault upon the decoy coach, Ike Holbeech's horse had been hit and he had flown over its head as it stumbled and fell dead. Although he was not the sharpest thinker one could hope to come across, it struck Holbeech powerfully that with a body of men banging away at them with rifles in that way, standing up would be in the nature of a badly advised course of action.

That being so, he just lay where he had fallen, hoping and praying that no horse would tread on him and stove in his skull. Luckily for him, this did not occur and after a time, both the sound of hoof-falls and rifle fire died away and there was silence.

Holbeech did not at first know what to do for the best. Being in doubt as to the best way to proceed, he decided that doing nothing at all might be the correct path to choose and so he just continued to lie there on his belly, with his head turned to one side. He observed men climbing down from the stagecoach and looking around the field of battle, whereupon Holbeech closed his eyes and carried on playing possum.

He could hear the men talking over the gunfight and joking about their success. Then he heard them discussing the fact that one man had escaped and talking of the need to pursue this man. Holbeech guessed that this was Ned Turner and he also deduced that Ned was probably heading back to Coopers Creek.

There was jingling of harness as the men uncoupled three of the horses from the stage and then tacked them up with their own saddles and bridles. There was a thunder of hoofs near by, and for the second time Ike Holbeech feared that a horse might be about to step on his head. Again, he was lucky.

All this while, Holbeech had barely dared to breathe, in case anybody noticed that he was not dead. The men who had been left behind seemed in no especial hurry to get on with their job. Instead, they rolled cigarettes and indulged in some self-congratulatory talk, which tended towards the conclusion that they were pretty fine fellows for fighting off a band of armed men in the way that they had. Holbeech seethed in fury.

Ridiculously, he felt that these men had behaved in a sly and dishonourable way by serving him and his fellow thieves so. Concealing themselves like that and then firing from cover! It was a scurvy, cowardly trick to play.

At length, the men began to search the bodies and collect up weapons. Holbeech had dropped the pistol that he had been holding when he fell off the horse, but he had another on his left hip. He opened his eyes a slit and saw that both men were going through the pockets of one of the other deputies. Whereupon Ike Holbeech sprang to his feet, drew his piece and shot both of the men dead before they even had the chance to register their surprise.

Feeling a sight better for having got some of his own back on those who had screwed up the raid on the stage,

Holbeech holstered his gun, picked up one of the repeating rifles from the coach and, after checking that it was loaded, set off on foot back towards Coopers Creek.

10

By the time that he had made peace with the miners and other men up at the diggings, Jack Crawley was feeling pretty braced with things in general. Before returning home, he had one final thing to do that day. His first port of call was the undertaker's shop.

Abe Calthorpe did not look best pleased to see him. 'I picked up Turner's body from the street. What do you want me to do with it?'

'Just hang on to it for a space. There are some men from the Pinkerton's agency who might want to take a look at it later. Do not worry, the town will pay the expenses, including a funeral if that is what happens.'

'If it happens? What the hell else can you be thinking of doing with a corpse, other than burying it?'

'I have an idea that those boys might

be wanting to take some of the dead from today's affair to claim rewards for them. I don't really know what they purpose.'

'You mean others were killed, beside Turner?'

'Yes, from what I am able to comprehend, all those so-called deputies of his have been killed.'

'That's a hell of a thing,' said Abe Calthorpe soberly.

'I guess,' said Crawley, 'that you know why I have come here?'

'Apart from talking of the disposal of Ned Turner's dead corpse, you mean? No, I could not venture a guess.'

'Abe, you and some others on that citizens' committee helped put Turner in power and then helped keep him there. I am thinking that you were scared, maybe he knew something about you that you would have rather kept secret. I don't know what that might be and do not wish to enquire. Truth is, neither you nor Jim Kincaid is fit to help run the town and I am looking for you to step down.'

'You are taking a heap upon yourself and no mistake. What if I refuse?'

'Then I shall have to make it a public matter, which I do not wish to do. Push me, though, and I shall do it. Just resign, Abe. This is the best I can do for you.'

Calthorpe thought the question over and then nodded.

* * *

Before he went to see Jim Kincaid with a similar request, Crawley thought it worth searching Turner's rooms above the Tanglefoot. He reached the saloon at just about the same time that Ike Holbeech came into sight of Coopers Creek.

For all his challenging of Ned Turner's authority, Holbeech was not a man who could really have headed any group of men engaged in any sort of enterprise. For one thing, he was not overburdened with brains; for another, he acted best when being given simple and clear instructions. This was why he had made a good right-hand man for Turner, but as soon as he had started initiating plans of his own, like the attack on the stage, things had ended up disastrously.

Holbeech had not had above a couple of dollars in his pocket when he went on that robbery, and he had no clear idea of what he would do if left to make decisions for himself. He wanted only to fix up again with Ned Turner and then they could get back to normal, with Ned working out what to do and he, Holbeech, following Ned's instructions. Crouched behind that rock outside of town now, Ike Holbeech felt very much alone and without any notion of what to do next, beyond finding Ned.

* * *

Jackson and the other two men had more or less worked out just what had taken place in their absence. Both the Pinkerton's men who had been left behind had been shot twice in the chest. Add to that the indisputable fact that there were only four dead robbers scattered around the stage and everything was plain as daylight.

'We had best get back to that little town and give them warning that things are not altogether settled just yet,' said Jackson. 'I will go on ahead. You men harness up the coach again and follow on, with all those men loaded up. I do not want to leave a rackful of 'Volcanics' here for anybody to help themselves. We have lost one already, now.

'You will not be able to bring the coach through the wood. I mind that there is a track up in that way, that turns off to the right after some miles. Do not take all day, I want this to be settled before dusk.'

* * *

It did not take Crawley long to find the weapon that had been used against Jim Kincaid. Turner had not made any great effort to hide the notes of hand signed by Kincaid. When he totalled up the amount, Jack Crawley shook his head sadly. Nearly $1,000! No wonder that Kincaid had not wished to oppose Turner's plans. This would have ruined the man.

There was nothing else of much interest in Turner's belongings, except for some papers relating to a town in California called Redemption. And, right at the bottom of the leather bag, tucked away in a corner so that he nearly missed it, there was a sheriff's star. It was of a slightly different design from the one that he himself was wearing. It was a fair guess that there was more to Ned Turner's past than any of them had known.

* * *

Holbeech was wholly at a loss to know what next to do. If Ned had returned to town, then presumably he would have gone back to his rooms over the saloon. All that he could think was that if only he could find Ned, then his old boss would make everything all right and come up with some new plan for their future.

Ike Holbeech began to work his way round the edge of the town, moving for cover from rock to tree, making his way to the back of the saloon. He had with him the rifle that he had taken from the rack in the stagecoach. When he was in plain sight of the saloon, he worked the lever, which chambered a cartridge at the same time as cocking the piece.

* * *

'Jack,' said Jim Kincaid, 'I surely am pleased to see you. You have had by all accounts a trying day. However, you have come through it without any harm and so I believe that I should be offering you my congratulations. I shall tell the committee that I think you should remain sheriff after this day. You are surely the best man for the job and I can't think what we were all about, voting in that Ned Turner.'

Judging from the rush of words, it was obvious that Kincaid was nervous and anxious to ingratiate himself with Crawley. Jack Crawley did not like to hear a man abase himself in this way. He cut short the flow of Kincaid's thanks, by saying, 'It's no manner of use, Jim, I know all about it.'

'About what? I have not the pleasure of understanding you, my old friend.'

Crawley pulled out the IOUs and laid them on the table.

'It's no use, Jim. I see now what Turner had over you. The best thing would be if you were to leave the citizens' committee and we will then forget about all this.'

'What? Then you too are blackmailing me?'

'I am not blackmailing you. The record of your debts to Turner lies there. You may burn it or do what you will. I do not want another scoundrel like Turner to get a toehold in my town. You and some others let him get a hold and so you are not the best man to be running the town. Just give it up and we can forget all about it.'

After some wrangling Kincaid agreed and it looked to Jack Crawley like he had done all that he could for one day.

* * *

Josie was sitting at her friend's house, waiting for Albert to be ready to come home. He was playing some complicated game with his schoolmate which involved charging up and down the stairs like a herd of buffalo.

'So your husband is now the sheriff after all?' said her friend.

'So it would appear,' replied Josie. 'Although I do not have a good understanding of the events of the day. Which is why I really will have to be taking Albert home now. I am expecting my husband home at any moment.'

'Lord, yes. I will go and call my son and tell him to bring Albert here directly.'

After another fifteen minutes of argument and complaint from the two boys, her son was ready to leave. Josie thanked her friend and she and Albert made their way home.

* * *

Ike Holbeech caused enormous consternation when he walked through the doors of the Tanglefoot. The bar-room was not busy, but those customers who were there were all talking excitedly about the astounding change which had taken place that day: Ned Turner being shot dead by the baker, who was in turn proclaimed the new sheriff. Not to mention where all Turner's friends had also seemingly been gunned down by Pinkerton's men.

It was in the middle of feverish conversation of this sort that one of those sitting facing the door to the street stopped speaking. His mouth quite literally dropped open in the most comical way imaginable. His drinking partner glanced round to see what could have caused this, and then his jaw also dropped and he too fell silent. Gradually, all those drinking in the saloon stopped talking and stared at the door, where Ike Holbeech stood with a rifle tucked under his arm.

The man whom they had all been assured was stone dead walked to the stairs which led to Turner's suite of rooms.

'Is Mr Turner at home?' he asked the barkeep. The man hardly knew what to reply and simply shrugged.

'What does that mean?' said Holbeech. 'Is Ned Turner up there or is he not?'

'He's over at Abe Calthorpe's place, I think,' said the barkeeper after thinking the matter over.

'What the hell is he doing at the

undertaker's?' asked Holbeech in bewilderment.

'Well, he's kind of deceased,' explained the man.

'That cannot be so. He was alive this morning. What has happened to him?'

'The sheriff shot him.'

'What are you talking about? Are you crazy or what? He *is* the sheriff. You mean he shot himself?'

'No sir, I mean the new sheriff, Mr Jack Crawley.'

Crawley! He might have guessed that that mealy-mouthed runt would have had a part in this. 'Where's Crawley now?'

'I don't rightly know. I think he was going over to see Jim Kincaid.'

Without another word Ike Holbeech charged like a bull from the saloon, leaving shocked amazement in his wake.

* * *

When Jackson returned to Coopers Creek after finding the bodies of his fellow agents, he began at once to look for a desperate man armed with a 'Volcanic' repeating rifle. All else apart, his job would be on the line if things went any more wrong than they already had. What had looked at first sight like a glorious victory, was swiftly degenerating into a possible catastrophe.

It did not take long for Geoffrey Jackson, Crawley's former sergeant and fellow veteran of the Mexican War to run Holbeech to earth. It happened by the purest chance as dusk was falling and Jackson was scrutinizing everybody in sight, wondering if any of them might have a repeating rifle concealed about their person.

Having seen nobody likely, he turned round and found himself face to face with an overweight man in early middle age, carrying one of the very distinctive 'Volcanic' rifles under his arm.

'Wait up, fellow,' said Jackson, moving his coat aside to give him easy access to the pistol at his side. 'I think you might have a piece of my property there.'

At this point, Holbeech raised the rifle and shot the Pinkerton's man at almost point-blank range.

Leastways, he had meant to shoot him, but so finely honed were Geoffrey Jackson's reactions after ten years in the army, five in the police and another five working for the Pinkerton's agency, that his arm was up, knocking away the barrel of the rifle before Holbeech could pull the trigger.

The bullet shot up into the evening sky. Ike Holbeech dropped the rifle and bolted across the street.

Jackson was feeling elated at his narrow escape, when the fleeing man turned and halted, pulled out his pistol and shot the Pinkerton's agent dead.

Crawley, who had met his wife and son on their way home, wondered what new devilment was afoot. He had not long to wait before finding out, because Holbeech came racing round the corner with his gun in his hand and, seeing the new sheriff pulling his pistol, Holbeech grabbed a hold of Albert and put his gun to the boy's head.

'You back off now, Crawley, or I swear to God I will kill the boy.'

'There's no call to do so,' said Crawley. 'Just let him go now and I will give you my oath to let you go as well. I will not pursue you.'

Even as he was speaking softly to the dangerous killer, Jack Crawley was sliding his pistol gently from the holster until it just hung there in his hand. Seeing this, Holbeech jerked the boy round sharply, so that he could more effectively use him as a shield.

Josie said, 'Please let my son go. He has no part in this, he is only a child.'

'That's as maybe,' said Holbeech. 'But that husband of yours has wrecked my life. He has left me with nothing.'

He began to edge away backwards, dragging the terrified boy with him. Jack Crawley just stood there as calm as a statue, saying and doing nothing that might provoke the man who held his son's life in his hands.

The two other Pinkerton's men came round the corner at this point, to one side of Holbeech and Crawley. They too had heard the gunfire and both had pistols in their hands.

'Put up those weapons,' said the sheriff. 'This is my call and you have no authority here.'

Reluctantly, the men holstered their guns. They stood there watching the unfolding drama, wondering how it would end.

All this time, Holbeech was backing away with the boy held in front of him. Albert was tall for his age and Ike Holbeech was pretty short, although somewhat tubby. The result was that the boy's body almost completely obscured Holbeech from view. It looked impossible that anybody would be able to shoot him without a good chance of hitting the boy.

And still he continued to back away; twenty feet, thirty feet, forty feet. When he was a good fifty feet from Crawley, his wife and the two Pinkerton's agents, Holbeech stopped to make his hold upon the boy more secure. He put his left arm round the child's throat and kept the pistol stuck right in his ear.

As Holbeech shifted position and was on the point of continuing to shuffle backwards, Jack Crawley raised both arms simultaneously. He bent his left elbow as he raised that arm and held the forearm in front of him at chest height. As he was doing this, he brought up his right hand, with the pistol in it, and rested it on the raised forearm for a fraction of a second, to steady his aim. Then he shot Ike Holbeech in the face, missing his son's own head by no more than two or three inches.

In the ensuing chaos, with his wife rushing over to enfold her child in her arms and various townsfolk arriving to see what the shooting was about, one of the Pinkerton's men came up to Crawley and held out his hand.

'That was the finest pistol shot I have

seen in some years. Fifty feet if it was an inch. Do you mind me asking what calibre that gun of yours is?'

'It's nominally 0.44,' said Crawley.

'Would you mind if I had a look at the weapon?' asked the man.

Crawley was aware that his wife would be justifiably angry with him over this whole business later, and since she seemed to be doing a reasonable enough job of soothing Albert and explaining what had happened to a sympathetic crowd, he did not suppose that his presence was called for immediately.

He pulled out the pistol and handed it to the other man, whose eyes widened in surprise.

'Colt Walker, hey? You don't see too many of these around. Special model too, I see. What's all this fancy engraving?' He held the pistol up close in the fading light and deciphered the inscription. 'Hero of Buena Vista? That would never be you, would it, my friend?'

Crawley shrugged modestly. 'It was a long time ago.' he said.

* * *

Some weeks after all this three men sat round a table at the Tanglefoot saloon, just shooting the breeze.

'That was a strange business, that day we woke up to find that we had not one but two sheriffs in the town.'

'Mark you,' said another, 'I am strongly of the opinion that we had only ourselves to blame for all that fuss and bother. Had we but voted in Jack Crawley in the first place, none of that blood would have been shed.'

'True,' said the man who had first spoken, 'but still and all, it all worked out well enough in the end.'

A third man said thoughtfully, 'It only goes to show that you can never tell about folk, just by what you see on the surface. Mark you though, it is few towns that have had two sheriffs at one and the same time, one then killing the other. If nothing else, it sets Coopers Creek aside from anywhere else.'

The three of them then poured another drink and the talk turned to other matters.

We do hope that you have enjoyed reading this large print book.

Did you know that all of our titles are available for purchase?

We publish a wide range of high quality large print books including:
Romances, Mysteries, Classics
General Fiction
Non Fiction and Westerns

Special interest titles available in large print are:
The Little Oxford Dictionary
Music Book, Song Book
Hymn Book, Service Book

Also available from us courtesy of Oxford University Press:
Young Readers' Dictionary
(large print edition)
Young Readers' Thesaurus
(large print edition)

For further information or a free brochure, please contact us at:
Ulverscroft Large Print Books Ltd.,
The Green, Bradgate Road, Anstey,
Leicester, LE7 7FU, England.
Tel: (00 44) **0116 236 4325**
Fax: (00 44) **0116 234 0205**

Other titles in the
Linford Western Library:

CALVERON'S CHASE

Caleb Rand

After five years inside Redrock Stockade, one-time US Marshal Jackson Calveron sets out on a manhunt — travelling hundreds of miles to find the men who had him falsely accused and convicted of manslaughter. But when he reaches the town of Las Cruces and finds himself embroiled in the aftermath of a brutal bank robbery, the death of a silver miner, and the machinations of criminals Fausto Salt and Copperhead Pintura, he begins to question his cause . . .

TRAIL TO ELSEWHERE

Walter L. Bryant

After seven-year-old Brad and his younger sister Julie are orphaned, they are separated and adopted by different families miles apart. As they grow up, each must face their own challenges: Brad's new brother Saul is hostile and brutal, while Julie, treated as a drudge, sees her only means of escape in marrying a man she does not love. Then Saul falls into criminality with the Coyote Gang. An altercation between the brothers lands Brad in jail — and Saul's path is about to cross with Julie's . . .

DARK MESA

Hank J. Kirby

Ross McCall is a rounder-up of maverick cattle for his own small herd. When he provides aid to wounded bandit Ace Morgan — last surviving member of an outlaw gang, and his pa's old comrade — the dying man repays his kindness by sharing the location of the band's last haul, hastily squirrelled away on McCall's land. But others are after the loot, imprisoning McCall and searching his his spread for the money. On his release, can McCall face down those who would snap up his land — and succeed in finding his legacy?

WHIRLWIND

Fenton Sadler

Hohanonivah — a Cheyenne orphan whose name means 'whirlwind' — is taken in as a child by Patrick and Esther Jackson, who raise him as their son. When, years later, his adoptive parents are murdered, Hohanonivah swears a solemn oath that those who took the elderly couple's lives will die by his hand. Tracking down the men responsible, he finds himself facing two of the most ruthless outlaws in the state — Jed and Eli Holt, psychopathic brothers who will kill for the most trifling of reasons . . .

THE OTHER CISCO KID

Sydney J. Bounds

When young Billy Baxter takes up with the Cisco Kid, the outlaw has a surprising proposition for him. Having been offered a marshal position in two separate towns, the Kid suggests that he and Baxter fill both vacancies between them — with Baxter youth assuming the Kid's identity, banking on the outlaw's reputation deterring would-be challengers. Eager for adventure, Baxter accepts, and takes up the star in Prospect. But he'll find that the town holds far more adventure than he'd bargained for . . .